'You are still a virgin...or am I imagining things?'

Emotions and responses running at storm-force strength, she stretched up to give him a forgiving kiss. That Roel should be her first lover was what she had always dreamt of. 'I didn't know I could feel like this...don't stop—'

Roel dropped a kiss on her brow. 'So... amazing virginal wife...is it possible that you are still almost a bride?'

Hilary paled and lowered her head. Of course he was now wondering if they were a newly married couple. She was so ashamed of herself that she couldn't look at him, and even less did she want to examine her own behaviour. Had she gone clean crazy?

'You're very quiet,' Roel remarked.

'Gosh, I'm dying for a shower!' Hilary exclaimed, and practically threw herself out of the bed.

BRIDES OF L'AMOUR

They triumph over tragedy—by finding lasting love…

Tabby, Pippa and Hilary: three friends whose lives were
changed for ever in their teens by a tragic accident. But
the wheel of fortune must turn up as well as down, and
these young women are about to get their share
of blessings…in the shape of three gorgeous men.
Christien, Andreo and Roel are all determined
to woo them and wed them…whatever that takes!

THE BANKER'S CONVENIENT WIFE

BY
LYNNE GRAHAM

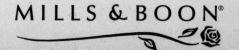

MILLS & BOON®

First published in Great Britain 2004
Harlequin Mills & Boon Limited,
Eton House, 18-24 Paradise Road, Richmond, Surrey TW9 1SR

© Lynne Graham 2004

ISBN 0 263 83719 X

Set in Times Roman 10½ on 12 pt.
01-0304-47459

Printed and bound in Spain
by Litografía Rosés, S.A., Barcelona

CHAPTER ONE

'NATURALLY you will not renew his contract. The Sabatino Bank has no place for inadequate fund managers.' Lean, dark, handsome face stern, Roel Sabatino was frowning. An international banker and a very busy man, he considered this conversation a waste of his valuable time.

His HR director, Stefan, cleared his throat. 'I thought…perhaps a little chat might put Rawlinson back on track—'

'I don't believe in little chats and I don't give second chances,' Roel incised with glacial effect. 'Neither—you should note—do our clients. The bank's reputation rests on profit performance.'

Stefan Weber reflected that Roel's own world-class renown as an expert in the global economy and the field of wealth preservation carried even greater impact. A Swiss billionaire, Roel Sabatino was the descendant of nine unbroken generations of private bankers and acknowledged by all as the most brilliant. Strikingly intelligent and hugely successful as he was, however, Roel was not known for his compassion towards employees with personal problems. In fact he was as much feared as he was admired for his ruthless lack of sentimentality.

Even so, Stefan made one last effort to intervene on the unfortunate member of staff's behalf. 'Last month, Rawlinson's wife walked out on him…'

'I am his employer, not his counsellor,' Roel countered in brusque dismissal. 'His private life is not my concern.'

That point clarified for the benefit of his HR director, Roel left his palatial office by his private lift to travel down to the underground car park. As he swung into his Ferrari his shapely masculine mouth was still set in a grim line of disdain. What kind of a man allowed the loss of a woman to interfere with his work performance to the extent of destroying a once promising career? A weak character guilty of a shameful lack of self-discipline, Roel decided with a contemptuous shake of his proud dark head.

A male who whined about his personal problems and expected special treatment on that basis was complete anathema to Roel. After all, by its very nature life was challenging and, thanks to a childhood of austere joylessness, Roel knew that better than most. His mother had walked out on her son and her marriage when he was a toddler and any suspicion of tender loving care had vanished overnight from his upbringing. Placed in a boarding-school at the age of five, he had been allowed home visits only when his academic results had matched his father's high expectations. Raised to be tough and unemotional, Roel had learnt when he was very young neither to ask for nor hope for favours in any form.

His car phone rang while he was stuck in Geneva's lunchtime traffic jam and regretting his decision not to utilise his chauffeur-driven limo. The call was from his lawyer, Paul Correro. When it came to more confidential matters, he preferred to utilise Paul's discreet services rather than those of the family legal firm.

'I think it's my duty as your legal representative to point out that the time has arrived for a certain connection to be quietly terminated.' Paul's tone was almost playful.

Roel had gone to university with Paul and he usually enjoyed the other man's lively sense of humour for nobody else would have dared that level of familiarity with him. However, he was not in the mood to engage in a guessing game.

'Cut to the chase, Paul,' he urged.

'I've been thinking of mentioning this for a while…' Unusually, Paul hesitated. 'But I was waiting for you to raise the topic first. It's almost four years now. Isn't it time to have your marriage of convenience dissolved?'

Taken aback by that reminder, and just when the traffic flow was finally beginning to move again, Roel lifted his foot off the clutch of his car. The Ferrari lurched to a sudden choking halt as the engine cut out and provoked a hail of impatient car horns that outraged Roel's masculine pride. But he did not utter a single one of the vituperative curses on the tip of his tongue.

From the car speakers Paul's well-modulated speaking voice continued in happy ignorance of the effect he had induced. 'I was hoping we could set up an appointment some time this week because I'll be on vacation from the following Monday.'

'This week is impossible for me,' Roel heard himself counter instantaneously.

'I hope I haven't overreached my remit in raising the issue,' Paul remarked with a hint of discomfiture.

'*Dio mio!* I had forgotten about the matter. You took me by surprise!' Roel proclaimed with a dismissive laugh.

'I didn't think it was possible to do that,' Paul commented.

'I'll have to call you back…the traffic's unbelievable,' Roel asserted and he concluded the dialogue without engaging in the usual chit-chat.

His handsome mouth was set in a taut line. Paul had been right to bring up the subject of the marriage, which Roel had felt he had little choice but to enter into almost four years earlier. How could he possibly have overlooked the necessity of breaking that slender link again with a divorce? He reminded himself that he led an incredibly busy life and thought back instead to the ridiculous situation that had persuaded him to circumvent the terms of his late grandfather's will with a fake wife.

His grandfather, Clemente, had been a rigid workaholic well into his sixties, in every way a chip off the rock like Sabatino banker block. But after his retirement Clemente had fallen in love with a woman less than half his age and had suffered a rebellious sea change in outlook. Throwing off all restraint, he had embraced New Age philosophies and had even briefly married the youthful gold-digger. His undignified behaviour had led to years of estrangement between Clemente and his son, Roel's conservative father. Roel himself, however, had retained his fondness for the older man and maintained contact with him.

Four years ago, Clemente had died and Roel had been incredulous when the terms of his grandfather's will had been spelt out to him. In that most eccentric document, Clemente had stated that in the event of his grandson failing to marry within a specified time frame, Castello Sabatino, the family's ancestral home, should devolve to the state rather than to his own flesh and blood. Certainly, Roel had lived to regret telling his grandfather that, as the chances of a happy marriage were in his own considered opinion slim to none, he would not be addressing the need to wed and father an heir until he was, at the very least, in late middle age.

Although Roel had been raised to scorn sentimentality, he had nonetheless still cherished dim childish memories of warm and happy visits to the Castello Sabatino. Although he was wealthy enough to buy a hundred ancient castles, he had learnt the hard way that the *castello* had an especially strong hold on his affections. Sabatinos had inhabited the castle, which stood high above a remote valley, for centuries and Roel had been appalled by the genuine threat of the property going out of the family, perhaps for ever.

A couple of months later, while he'd been in London on business, he had been using his mobile phone to discuss with Paul the almost insurmountable problems created by his grandfather's will. Even though he had been in a public place at the time, indeed he had been getting a haircut, he had assumed that the very fact that the conversation was taking place in Italian had meant that it was almost as private as it might have been in his office. He had learnt that he was mistaken when his little hair-stylist had leapt headlong into his private conversation to first commiserate with him over his grandfather's 'weirder than weird' will and, second, to offer up herself as a 'pretend' wife so that he could keep Castello Sabatino in the family.

Ultimately, Hilary Ross had sold her hand in marriage to him in a straight business deal. What age would she be now? Roel mused. Twenty-three years

old last St Valentine's Day, his memory supplied
without hesitation. He was willing to bet that she still
didn't look much older than a teenager. She was very
small but wonderfully curvaceous and back then at
least her dress sense had rested on the extreme gothic
edge of fashion. Black from head to foot, clumpy
boots and vampire make-up, he recalled with a frowning smile rather than a shudder. It was strange how
very sexy a vampire could look, he reflected abstract-
edly. Before the traffic lights could change, he dug
out his wallet and with long, deft fingers extracted the
snapshot Hilary had pressed on him. A snapshot
adorned with a teasing signature, 'Your wife, Hilary,'
and backed by her phone number.

'Something to remember me by,' she had said, bab-
bling like a brook in flood because he had known and
she had somehow sensed that, aside of any necessary
legal need to keep tabs on her whereabouts, he would
not seek any further personal contact with her.

'Kiss me,' those huge eyes of hers had pleaded in
a silent invitation.

Resolute to the last, he had withstood temptation.
They had had a business arrangement that had to remain unsullied by sex: Paul had made it clear to him
that if he'd consummated what had essentially been
only a marriage on paper he would have made himself
liable for a substantial maintenance claim.

He must have imagined being tempted by her, Roel
told himself in exasperation. What possible appeal
could she have had for him? She had left school at
sixteen. She was an uneducated girl from a poor
working-class background. *Dio mio*…a hairdresser! A
giggly little hairdresser, only five feet plus in height
and wholly without cultural interests or sophistica-

tion! They had had only their humanity in common. Finally he allowed himself to glance down at the photograph. She wasn't beautiful, he reminded himself, exasperated by his own disturbing absorption in such thoughts. He drew his own attention to the fact that her brows were too straight and heavy, her nose a little too large. But regardless of her flaws his brilliant dark gaze still locked to the impish look of fun in her eyes and the wide, bright smile curving her lush mulberry-painted mouth.

'When I worked as a junior on Saturdays, I used to blow every penny I earned on shoes,' she had once confided unasked and in much the same way he had picked up other titbits and glimpses of a lifestyle as far removed from his own as that of an alien.

'When my grandma met my grandpa, she said she knew he was the love of her life before they even spoke…anyway, they *couldn't* speak. She didn't know a word of English and he didn't know a word of Italian. Don't you think that's romantic?'

He had considered it beneath his dignity to respond. In fact he had stonewalled all her attempts to flirt with him. So he was a snob, socially and intellectually, but she had not been from his world. Furthermore he was all too well acquainted with the Sabatino male habit of marrying gold-diggers and far too clever to risk following in his father's and his grandfather's footsteps to make the same crucial mistake. He had suppressed what he had recognised as an inappropriate and dangerous attraction to an unsuitable woman.

Yet he still couldn't forget the last time that he had seen his fake wife: her jaunty wave in spite of the suspicious glisten in her eyes, the gritty, defiant smile that had told him that she was going to find a guy who *did* believe in romance…had she found that mythical male? Discovered his feet of clay? Was that why she had yet to request a divorce on her own behalf?

In the act of wondering that while rounding a notorious bend, Roel only had a split second to react when a child ran off the pavement into the road in pursuit of a dog. Braking hard, he wrenched at the steering wheel in a ferocious attempt to avoid hitting the little girl. The Ferrari smashed nose first into the wall on the other side of the street with a bone-numbing jolt, but he would still have walked unhurt from the wreckage had he had the chance to get out of his car before another vehicle crashed into it. As that second collision followed a blinding pain burst at the base of Roel's skull and plunged him into darkness.

The photograph still curled within fingers that refused to relinquish their grip, he was rushed into hospital. His late father's sister, Bautista, was called to the emergency room. With haughty scorn, Bautista watched two young nurses react to Roel's extravagant dark good looks with hungry eyes of awe.

A spoilt and imperious brunette dressed in a style that the less charitable might have judged inappropriate for a woman of sixty, Bautista was furious at the interruption to her day. Roel would be fine! Roel was indestructible; all the Sabatino men were. Aside of the blow to his head, his other injuries were minor. The following day, Bautista was due to fly to Milan to attend a gallery opening with her fiancé, Dieter, and she was determined not to change her plans.

Only ten days earlier, Roel had infuriated her with

the information that the handsome young sculptor
whom she was planning to marry had a history of
chasing wealthy older women. How horribly insulting
Roel had been! Why shouldn't Dieter want her for
herself? Bautista was confident that she was still a
remarkably good-looking woman, possessed of a
most engaging personality. Four staggeringly expensive divorces had failed to diminish her shining faith
in love and matrimony.

When a consultant finally came to Bautista to tell
her that, although Roel had recovered consciousness,
he appeared to be suffering from some degree of temporary amnesia, her annoyance and subsequent frustration were intense.

'Is Mr Sabatino's wife on her way?' Bautista was
then asked.

'He's not married.'

With a look of surprise the older man extended a
somewhat crumpled photograph to her. 'Then who is
this?'

In astonishment, Bautista studied the photo and its
revealing inscription. Roel had married an
Englishwoman? My goodness, how secretive he had
been! But then was he not *famed* for his cold reserve
and reticence? His extreme dislike of publicity? His
marriage would indeed excite the kind of headlines
that he would consider to be distasteful and intrusive,
Bautista conceded. Exactly when had he been planning to inform his relatives that he had taken a wife?
But at that point happily appreciating that Roel's pos-
session of a wife freed her from all further responsibility for him while he lay in his hospital bed,
Bautista rushed off to phone her nephew's mystery
bride.

The instant Hilary walked into her tiny flat and saw her sister Emma's troubled face, a cold shiver trickled down her spine.

'What's wrong?' Hilary asked, hastily setting down the evening paper she had gone out to buy.

'While you were out, a woman phoned…I want you to sit down before I pass on her news.' Emma was a tall slender blonde with a steady look in her grey eyes that hinted at an unusual degree of maturity for a girl of seventeen.

Hilary frowned. 'Don't be daft. You're here and all in one piece and the only family I've got. Who phoned…and with what news?'

'I'm not the only family you've got,' her sister said in a strained undertone. 'Roel…Roel Sabatino has been involved in a car accident.'

The blood slowly draining from her cheeks, Hilary stared back at the younger woman with stricken eyes. Her legs wobbled beneath her and she swayed. 'He's—?'

'Alive…*yes*!' A supportive arm curving to Hilary's slight shoulders, Emma urged her smaller sister down onto the small sofa in the kitchen that also had to serve as a sitting and dining area. 'Roel's aunt phoned. She spoke very little English and she only called for about two minutes max—'

'How badly has he been hurt?' Hilary was trembling and feeling sick. Her mind was a blank and then suddenly a frightening sea of disturbing images. Even as she strained to hear Emma's response she was praying that that response would offer some hope.

'He has some kind of head injury. I got the impression that it might be serious. He's being transferred to another hospital and I did make sure that I got the details.' Emma squeezed her sister's hand in a bracing gesture. 'Take a slow deep breath, Hilly. Concentrate on the fact that Roel's alive. You're in shock but you can be with him by tomorrow morning.'

Bowing her swimming head, Hilary was half in a world of her own. Roel, the precious secret love of her life—even if she had not been anything more than a useful means to an end for him. It was strange and terrifying how love could strike like that, Hilary reflected, gripped by a momentary agony of regret. Roel, the husband of her heart, whom she had never even kissed. Roel, so tall and dark and vitally strong, who right this minute might be fighting for his life in a hospital bed. Her skin clammy with fear for him, she prayed that he would recover but it was a big challenge for Hilary to be optimistic on such a score. Almost seven years earlier, the car crash that had killed both her mother and their father had shattered her and Emma's lives. On that occasion, the long nerve-racking wait at the hospital concerned had not resulted in any last-minute miracle survivals.

'Be with him?' Hilary echoed belatedly. '*Be*…with Roel?'

Could she be with him…dared she try? Wild hope leapt up inside Hilary. She might be his wife in name only but that did not mean that she could not be concerned about his well-being. Hadn't his aunt called to tell her about his accident? Obviously their marriage was not the secret she had assumed it would be within his family circle. It seemed evident too that his relative believed that theirs was something more than a marriage on paper.

'I knew that every minute counted and I knew exactly what you'd want to do,' Emma hastened to assure her. 'This is an emergency. So, I went straight on to the Internet and booked a flight to Geneva for you. It leaves first thing tomorrow—'

With an effort, Hilary parted dry lips and strove to temper her desperate desire to rush to Roel's side with a little common sense. 'Of course I want to go to him but—'

'No buts…' Her dismay palpable and her voice betraying a sharp edge of strain, Emma leapt upright. 'Don't be too proud to rush over there to be with Roel. You're his wife and I bet that what you once had together could still be mended. I'm old enough now to appreciate just how much trouble my bad attitude must've caused between the two of you!'

Hilary was very much taken aback by that explosive speech. Until that moment, she had had no idea that Emma might have blamed herself for the apparent breakdown of her sister's marriage. 'My relationship with Roel just didn't work out. You mustn't think that you had the *slightest* thing to do with that,' she stressed in awkward protest.

'Stop trying to protect me.' Emma groaned. 'I was a selfish little madam. We'd lost Mum and Dad and I was so possessive of you that you were afraid to even let me meet Roel!'

Registering with a sinking heart that every lie, even one that had once seemed like a little white harmless lie, would eventually exact its punishment, Hilary could no longer look the younger woman in the eye. 'It wasn't like that between Roel and me,' she began uncomfortably.

'Yes, it was. You put me first and let me spoil your wedding day and ruin your marriage before it even got off the ground. I was horribly rude to Roel and I threatened to run away if you tried to make me live abroad. I came between the two of you…of course I did!' Emma sucked in a steadying breath. 'You were so much in love with him. I still can't believe how cruel I was to you…'

Hilary had to struggle to concentrate on the unexpected angle the dialogue had taken, for the greater percentage of her thoughts was anxiously lodged on the state of Roel's health. Resolving to sort out her sister's unfortunate misapprehensions at a more suitable time, she prompted, 'What exactly did Roel's aunt say?'

'That he was asking for you,' Emma lied, crossing two sets of fingers behind her back as though to apologise for a fib that she hoped would make her sister feel more confident about flying out to be with her estranged husband.

Roel was asking for her? Surprise that was overwhelmed by a surge of pure joy washed over Hilary and, suddenly, she felt equal to any challenge. She would walk on fire for him, swim lakes, climb the very mountains to reach his side. Roel *needed* her! That knowledge cut through every barrier like a knife through butter. If a male of Roel's intimidating self-sufficiency could express a wish for her presence, however, he had to be very weak or seriously ill, Hilary decided worriedly. She hurried into her bedroom to pack.

'But the salon,' she groaned, rifling the wardrobe for essential clothes and barely able to think straight. 'Who'll look after it?'

'Sally,' her sister suggested, referring to Hilary's second-in-command at the hair salon, Sally Witherspoon. 'You said she was brilliant when you had the flu.'

In the dimly lit hall, Hilary snatched up the phone, eyes an abstracted but luminous grey. The silky hair that framed her oval face shone bright as a beacon. It was that gleaming shade of silvery fairness most often achieved by artificial means. Times without number, Hilary had been forced to explain to disbelieving customers that her hair was natural. Perhaps as an apology for not having had to resort to the permanents and the bleach so beloved of her clientele, she occasionally added a faint hint of another colour to the tips of her hair and this particular month she had employed a pale and delicate hue of pink.

She arranged for Sally to collect the salon keys and phoned another stylist who occasionally came in when things were busy to offer the woman full-time work during her own absence. Those practicalities dealt with, she refused to even think about how all such extra costs would eat into her already tight profit margins. She focused on her sister, Emma, and winced. 'How can I leave you here alone in the flat?'

'My half-term break is over tomorrow and I'll be catching the train back to school anyway,' her sister pointed out. 'I hope I can manage that for myself. I'm seventeen, Hilly.'

Embarrassed by that reminder, Hilary gave the sister she adored an emotional hug.

With hindsight, she could only marvel at the difference that time and Roel's financial rescue package had made to both their lives. She owed Roel so much. In truth, she owed him a debt she could never repay!

Four years ago, the sisters had been living in a dingy flat on a crime-ridden council estate and life had been bleak. Emma had always been clever and Hilary had been determined to ensure that the tragic early death of their parents did not prevent the younger girl from achieving her full academic potential. Hilary had been devastated by a guilty sense of failure when her kid sister had fallen in with the wrong company and started playing truant from school. At the time, Hilary had been working long hours as a junior stylist. She had been in no position to afford either a move to a better area or to spend more time supervising a rebellious teenager.

Roel's generosity had turned their lives around. She hadn't wanted to accept his money but she had realised that that money would give her the best possible chance of setting her little sister back on the straight and narrow path again. She had spent only what it took to set up her own hairdressing business in the far from fashionable London suburb of Hounslow. Taking into account Emma's needs at the time, Hilary believed that she had made the right decision. Only, sometimes, she would still find herself wondering if Roel would have lowered his guard, respected her more and even retained contact with her had she *stuck* to her original intention of simply marrying him and refusing any reward whatsoever.

After all, she had meant to marry him in the same guise as that of a friend doing him a favour. Besotted beyond belief as she had been with Roel, a guy who had hardly seemed to know that she was alive, she would have done almost anything to please or impress him. But sadly, once she had succumbed to the lure of allowing his wealth to solve her problems, once she had taken his money, she had changed everything between them, she conceded unhappily.

'I prefer to pay for services rendered,' Roel had drawled and he had made her feel horribly like a hooker. 'That way there's no misunderstanding.'

Mid-morning the following day, Dr Lerther strove to conceal his surprise when his secretary ushered in Roel Sabatino's wife, Hilary. The tiny blonde woman whose anxiety was writ large in her bright grey eyes was in no way what he had expected.

'I did try to phone before I left the UK but the operator couldn't find the number for this place,' Hilary confided in an explanatory rush.

She was very nervous. The last word in opulence, the hospital was like no other she had ever entered and she had had to advance considerable evidence of her identity before she'd even been allowed in. Her increasingly desperate requests just for word of Roel's condition had been repeatedly met with polite but steely blankness. Baulked of her expectation that Roel's aunt, Bautista, would be waiting to greet her and smooth her passage, she had been forced to introduce herself as Roel Sabatino's wife. Having done so, she felt horribly dishonest but she was convinced that were she to tell the truth about their marriage, she would not even be allowed to visit Roel.

'This is a private clinic and as our patients demand discretion and security, the number is not freely available.' The grey-haired older man extended his hand. 'I'm relieved that you were able to get here so quickly—'

Reading dire meaning into that assurance, Hilary turned pale as milk and gasped, 'Roel?'

'I'm sorry; I didn't mean to worry you. Physically, aside of a severe headache, your husband is suffering

from nothing more than a few bruises.' With a soothing smile the consultant swept her across his luxurious office into a seat. 'However, his memory has not
been so fortunate.'

The worst of her apprehension set to rest and weak
with relief, Hilary sank down into the armchair and
then looked puzzled. 'His…er…memory?' ·

'Mr Sabatino suffered a blow to the head and he
was unconscious for some hours. A degree of disorientation is not unusual after such an episode…
unfortunately, in this case, there seems to be some
temporary impairment of the memory system.'

Alerted by the older man's air of gravity, Hilary
had become very still. 'Meaning?' she pressed, dry-
mouthed.

'A standard examination after he first recovered
consciousness at the hospital revealed a discrepancy
in his perception of dates—'

'Dates?' Hilary queried again.

'Roel's memory has misplaced what I estimate to
be the past five years of his life. He himself was un-
aware that there was a problem until it was pointed
out to him. He is fully in control of every aspect of
his past as it was *then*, but all events since that time
are a closed book to him.'

Hilary stared back at the older man in shaken disbelief. 'Five whole…*years*? Are you certain of this?'

'Of course. Mr Sabatino has no memory of the car
crash either.'

'But why has this happened to him?' Hilary asked
worriedly.

'It is not that unusual for there to be a degree of
memory loss as a result of a head injury but as a rule
only very small spaces of time are involved. It is

called retrograde amnesia. Occasionally emotional trauma or even stress may lead to such an episode but I think we may discount that possibility in this particular case,' Dr Lerther opined with confidence. 'It is almost certainly a temporary condition and within hours or even days what has been forgotten will be recalled either in parts or, indeed, all at once.'

'How is Roel taking this?' Hilary asked weakly.

'Once your husband realised how much time his mind has effectively omitted from his recollection he was very shocked.'

'I bet…' Hilary was struggling to imagine how Roel, who took for granted that he should be one hundred per cent in control of himself and everything around him, would cope with a huge big spanner being thrown in the works.

'Prior to that revelation, Mr Sabatino was on the brink of ignoring all medical advice and returning to his office,' Dr Lerther admitted ruefully. 'For a man of such strong character and intellect, indeed a man accustomed to wielding considerable power, an inexplicable event may be a very frustrating challenge to accept.'

An expression of profound dismay had set Hilary's mobile features as she worked out the ramifications of the five years that the older man had chosen to describe as being simply, 'misplaced'. 'For goodness' sake…Roel won't even remember me!'

'I was leading up to that point,' the consultant asserted in a bracing tone. 'But I'm most relieved that you're here to give Mr Sabatino the support he needs to deal with this situation—'

Her brow had pleated. 'Isn't Roel's aunt Bautista here too?'

'I understand that the lady left the country this morning to attend a pressing social engagement,' Dr Lerther advanced.

Astonished by that information, Hilary swallowed hard on an exclamation. So much for Auntie Bautista! Evidently there was little family affection to hope for from that quarter. Her own head was swimming with a mess of conflicting promptings. At first reassured by the news that Roel was not seriously hurt, she had been thrown right out of her depth when informed of his loss of memory. She tried to picture waking up to her own world as it had been five years earlier rather than as it was now. Even in trying to take fleeting account of all the many changes that had taken place since then in her life, she reached a more disturbing appreciation of just how disorientating Roel's condition would be for him.

She was disgusted by his aunt's uncaring attitude but not that surprised for she and her sister had once endured similar indifference from a close relative. She thought of the debt that she still felt she owed Roel and of how much she wanted to see him. In a purely disinterested and friendly way, she could be of help and support to him. It was an innately tantalising and seductive idea. But wouldn't it be dishonest to pose as his *real* wife? She was his wedded wife in name but in no other way.

A quiver of shamed distaste at the concept of letting such a lie stand slivered through Hilary's slight frame. However, she had promised Roel that she would never, ever reveal the true terms of their marriage to anybody and, to ease her conscience, she decided to tell a half-truth instead. 'I should admit that

Roel and I have been…er…estranged,' she said awkwardly.

'I thank you for your confidence and I assure you that what you have told me will go no further. But I must also ask you not to reveal *any* potentially distressing facts to my patient if you can avoid doing so,' the older man emphasised with considerable gravity. 'Although your husband will not acknowledge it, he is already under great stress and adding to that burden could endanger his full recovery.'

As that hard reality was spelt out to her Hilary lost colour and nodded in earnest understanding. From her lips, Roel would learn nothing that might upset him.

'As Mr Sabatino's wife, you are his next of kin and you may do what others may not for his benefit. He has countless employees; those he pays to do his bidding but mercifully you are in a much stronger position,' Dr Lerther opined cheerfully. 'Your husband needs to feel that he has someone close whom he can trust. Make no mistake. His present state makes him vulnerable.'

'I can't imagine Roel being vulnerable.' Hilary's throat was thick with tears and she could no longer meet the consultant's kindly gaze. She was all too painfully aware that she too fell into the demeaning category of being someone whom Roel had once paid to carry out his wishes. But she was also devastated by the obvious fact that he should have nobody other than her available to take on such a role.

'Nonetheless, if I may speak freely…it will be your responsibility to stand between him and all those business personnel who will seek access to him. His own needs must be put first,' Dr Lerther advised her. 'The Sabatino Bank must survive without him at present.

He requires rest and relaxation. I am also sufficiently acquainted with the world financial markets to be conscious that no hint of Mr Sabatino's current condition should go beyond this room.'

Hilary's brow had furrowed for she had not even a passing acquaintance with the state of the world financial markets. She had no grasp whatsoever of that aspect of Roel's existence and very little interest in the matter either. Instead, with innate practicality she had homed in on what would plainly be her own role. It would be her duty to look after Roel until such time as he regained his memory.

'May I see him now?'

The consultant recalled his patient's initially appalled reaction to the discovery that he was a married man and hastily suppressed the image of a loving little Christian being thrown to the lions. Hilary Sabatino could well be more resilient than she appeared. She might even be capable of standing firm against the glacial freeze of her billionaire husband's despotic and wholly intimidating character...but even if Dr Lerther had been a gambling man, he would not have risked a bet on that outcome.

Hilary breathed in deep and followed in the nurse's wake. In just minutes she would see the only male who had ever managed to make her cry...

CHAPTER TWO

A WIFE, Roel thought morosely.

Was it any wonder his memory had chosen to betray him by overlooking the most unprofitable acquisition in a man's life since the advent of disease? Although he was only in his thirtieth year, it seemed that he had already sacrificed his freedom. Just as his father had done and his father before him: marry young, repent in millions. Yet he had sworn to himself that he would not make the same error.

He had steered clear of messy personal entanglements and kept mistresses who excelled between the sheets instead. He had a high sex drive, so he took care of it. Lust could not control him. Nor had he ever believed in love. So, love could thankfully have had nothing to do with his evident change of heart on the matrimonial front.

Certain things, however, he did not require memory to know. Indeed certain things he knew by instinct. The wife, whom his undisciplined mind had chosen to forget, would be a tall, elegant brunette because that was the type of woman who attracted him. She would be from a wealthy background and possessed of impeccable society lineage. She might be a career woman—a banker or even an economist, a possibility that was of some small comfort to him. Perhaps while discussing risk management and investment strategy he had recognised a working soul mate. An unemotional and otherwise quiet woman, who would respect

the demands of his schedule when he was too busy
to see her.

A knock sounded on the door. He swung round
from the window, a male who stood six feet four
inches, broad of shoulder and lean of hip, his tall,
well-built frame sheathed in an Armani business suit
of faultless cut.

'Will you close your eyes before I come in?' a low-
pitched British voice asked. 'Cos if you don't I'm
likely to feel really silly introducing myself to you as
a wife.'

Shock one…he had married a foreigner with a de-
finable regional accent rather than the clear flattened
vowel sounds of the English upper class. Shock
two…she used teenage slang and made childish requests.

'Roel?' Hilary prompted in the taut silence.

Raw impatience clenched Roel's even white teeth
together. He recognised that there were two ways of
playing the scene. Either he could blast her out before
she even came through the door or he could play
along until such time as he had worked out exactly
who and what he was dealing with. 'OK…'

'I suppose you're really nervous about this too but,
now that I'm here, you don't need to worry about
anything any more.'

His back turned to the door, his dark deep-set eyes
alight with intense disbelief, Roel actually found himself snatching in a sustaining breath. Shock three…he
had married a woman who, in the space of a mere
sixty seconds, could contrive to antagonise and offend
him by treating him with disrespect.

'I was just so touched that you were asking for me
at the hospital…' Hilary gabbled, hastening in and

closing the door behind her and only then daring to open her own eyes.

'I *asked* for you?' Roel questioned with incredulity. 'How could I have asked for you when I don't remember you?'

'My goodness, what are you doing out of bed?' Hilary demanded in astonishment, losing all track of what they had been talking about.

'Tell me, do you work using a list of stupid comments or do they come to mind without effort?' Roel shot back with sardonic bite as he swung round to face her.

Standing upright and only three feet from her, Roel's sheer size was menacing. She had to tilt her head back to get a proper look at him and then, even though she had flinched at that cutting comeback, she could not take her attention from him. Her mouth ran dry and her heartbeat speeded up for before her stood the living, breathing male embodiment of her every desire and dream.

The stark male beauty of his lean dark features hit her with explosive force. He was incredibly good-looking and shockingly sexy. But he also had a magnetic presence of command and icy authority that she could feel right down to the marrow of her bones. He did not smile and she wasn't surprised. His charismatic smile was rare and the chill in the room was pronounced. And she understood, she understood even his aggressive attack on her, and her heart twisted inside her with loving forgiveness. Torture could not have dragged the truth from him but she knew that he was as close to scared as he was ever likely to be. She was well aware that the sudden onslaught of a forgotten wife was probably his worst nightmare come true.

'I don't like sarcasm,' she told him, tilting up her chin.

'I don't like stupid questions.' Roel discovered that he had to lower the angle of his gaze even to bring his wife into his field of vision. She was tiny but not remotely doll-like, very much an individual and only in her early twenties at most, he noted, succumbing to grudging fascination. Her grey eyes were the colour of stormy seas. Her hair was a shimmering silvery blonde worn in a short spiky cut and tipped with pink. *Pink?* It had to be a trick of the light, he decided. She had a smattering of freckles across her nose and luscious cherry-red lips that would have tempted a saint.

The distinct tightening in his groin caught Roel by surprise for he was long past the teenage years when his body had last cast off his disciplined control. But as his attention roamed down over his wife's glorious hourglass shape his arousal only became more pronounced. Full, rounded breasts were moulded by a blue cotton tee shirt while low-slung hipster jeans accentuated her tiny waist and the pronounced curve of her highly feminine hips. While his rational mind struggled to name shock four in his encounter with his wife as her total lack of exclusive designer elegance, his appreciative hormones were winning hands down. He might not remember her but the dynamite sexual charge she ignited in him spoke a great deal louder than memory or words. Roel always had to explain the inexplicable and he was now satisfied as to why he must have married her.

'I think you should still be resting.' Involuntarily, Hilary connected with smouldering dark golden eyes and what little grasp she had on the muted dialogue vanished.

'Are you in the habit of telling me what to do?' Roel enquired, striving for a warning note that ended up unaccountably husky.

'What do you think?' As she met his stunning gaze her mouth ran dry and her tummy flipped. The atmosphere sizzled and her whole body leapt with energised awareness. No matter how hard she tried she couldn't drag in enough oxygen to fill her lungs. Her bra felt too tight, her breasts full and sensitive. Her nipples pinched tight and stung, reacting to the same sensual heat that was flaring into wicked being deep within her pelvis. She knew exactly what was happening to her and, worse, that she was powerless to stop it. This was, after all, the guy who had almost sunk her to the degrading level of offering up her virginity for a no-strings-attached one-night stand. She had craved Roel that much and that bad and, had he displayed any interest in that direction, pride would not have held her back.

Exercising the fierce strength of will that was the backbone of his character, Roel removed his intent gaze from his wife. So at least he understood why he had married a youthful sex kitten with no dress sense: lust, mindless, rampant lust, he labelled, his handsome masculine mouth hardening. He was appalled that he could have been that predictable but not one to beat himself up over a sin of the flesh.

'The woman who tried to tell me what to do would be a fool,' Roel murmured with smooth, cutting cool. 'I'm sure you don't fall in that category.'

'I don't squash easy either,' Hilary told him doggedly, her colour high but her spine rigid as she utilised every scrap of dignity she possessed to rise above the humiliating weakness of her own body. 'After what you've been through, you should still be in bed.'

His beautifully shaped ebony brows drew together in a fleeting frown line. 'I have no further need for medical attention. I'm sorry if you have been concerned but I'm heading back into the office.'

Her eyes widened to their fullest extent. 'You can't be serious.'

'As I am rarely anything else, I cannot imagine why you should suggest otherwise. Or believe that I'm likely to be in need of your opinion on the issue,' Roel sliced back in glacial dismissal.

'Well, for what it's worth, I'm going to give you my opinion unasked,' Hilary slammed back at him angrily. 'Maybe you think it's dead macho to act like there's nothing wrong with you but I just think that that's plain stupid!'

Dark golden eyes flared, incandescent with anger. 'I—'

'You're suffering from a very worrying loss of memory and you are not thinking through what you are doing—'

Roel flung his proud dark head high. 'I never act without thought—'

'By going back to work, you would be denying that there's even a problem. I can't let you do that—'

'Tell me one thing,' Roel countered with sardonic clarity. 'Before the car smash, were we in the process of divorce?'

'Not that I know of!' Hilary tossed back, small hands spreading on her hips to maintain a firmer grip, her grey eyes bright with resolve. 'You may be a very clever guy but you can also be very stubborn and extremely impractical. Right now, it's my job to make sure that you don't do *anything* that you'll later regret, so get back in that bed and take it easy!'

Brilliant eyes enhanced by black spiky lashes, Raul surveyed her as though she were a madwoman in need of restraint. 'Nobody tells me what to do. I'm astonished that you should think that you have the right to impose your views on me.'

'Yeah, marriage is a toughie for a control freak,' Hilary slammed back unimpressed. 'I'm not about to apologise for trying to protect you from yourself. If you go back into the bank, your employees will realise that there's something wrong with you—'

'There is nothing wrong with me, only a temporary phase of *slight* disorientation—'

'During which you forgot about a great fat chunk of your past life!' Hilary slotted in heatedly. 'I think that's very relevant and a lot more dangerous than you're prepared to admit. There'll be employees and clients you won't even recognise, situations you don't understand and which you may screw up. You're also five flipping years out of date with your precious work. Who are you planning to take into your confidence in an effort to avoid making embarrassing mistakes? Because one thing I *do* know about you, Roel…just about the only person alive whom you trust is yourself!'

Out of breath and trembling with the force of her feelings, for she was aghast at the very idea of him attempting an immediate return to work, Hilary glared at Roel in challenge. Just as quickly her expression changed to one of anxiety as she saw him frown as though with pain. Only then did she register the ashen

cast of his complexion and the slight tremor in his
hand as he raised it to his head.

'Sit down...' Closing both hands over his, Hilary
urged him back towards the armchair behind him.

Roel was swaying but he still fought her attempt
to help him. 'But I don't need—'

'Shut up and sit down!' Hilary launched at him
fiercely and she used his uneven balance to topple
him down into the chair like a felled tree.

'*Per meraviglia...*' Roel groaned in frustration.
'It's only a headache.'

But Hilary had already hit the call button to bring
a nurse and the presence of that third party, soon followed by the entry of Dr Lerther, prevented Roel
from expressing his fury at her interfering and taking
charge in such a way.

In any case, Roel had recognised that his wife had
panic written all over her. He decided that there was
something to be said for a woman with a face that
seemed to wear her every passing thought. Her eyes
were dark with stress and worry and she stood humbly
at the back of the room, demonstrating what he considered to be exaggerated respect for the medical personnel while nibbling anxiously at a nail.

He couldn't take his attention off his nail-biting
wife. She looked so scared on his behalf and she was
trembling. Concern for his health must have made her
shout at him. She seemed to be fond of him. She
might well be fonder still of his immense wealth and
all that it could buy her, Roel conceded cynically but,
indisputably, she seemed to cherish some degree of
genuine fondness for him. He knew all women were
terrific actresses but any single one of the previous

lovers he could recall would have withstood torture sooner than succumb to cannibalising a nail.

In addition his wife was neither as uncomplicated nor as predictable as he had initially assumed. A startling amount of fire and defiance lurked behind that cute and curvaceous feminine exterior. He was accustomed to women who said yes to his every request and worked hard at meeting his expectations before he could even be put to the trouble of voicing a request. He had never met a woman who had the nerve to shout at him or one who would go toe to toe with him in a fight. In actuality, he did not argue with people *ever*. He had never had to argue. Arguments just didn't happen to him.

Hilary was feeling hugely, *horribly* guilty and shaken up. Roel was still suffering from the physical after-effects of a serious accident and she had lost her temper with him. How could she have done that? As a rule she had an even temper and a sunny easygoing nature. What had come over her? Instead of being calm and coaxing and patient, she had been strident and emotional and accusing. He had looked taken aback. She didn't think he was used to being shouted at and she could not believe that she had done so.

Sucking in a deep steadying breath, she studied him. Her heart jumped as though it were on a trampoline. His luxuriant black hair was tousled, bold profile taut, his dense black lashes cut crescent-shaped shadows over his proud olive cheekbones. Extravagantly handsome, he had a raw masculine appeal that turned female heads wherever he went. He still took her breath away. Just as he had the very first time she'd seen him and the recollection of that particular day nearly four years ago swept her back in time…

Talking on a mobile phone, Roel had walked through the door of the busy salon where she'd worked as a junior stylist. There he had stilled, ebony brows elevating with a faint air of well-bred surprise as he'd taken in his surroundings. She had immediately understood that, like others before him, he had mistaken the salon for the much more exclusive place a few doors further along the street. In that split second when he had been on the brink of wheeling round to leave again something had propelled her forward. Something? The fact that he was so outrageously good-looking she would have gone without food for a week just to own a photo of him? How could she explain her own unbelievably powerful need to prevent him walking back out of her life again as casually as he had wandered into it?

'Just you stay on the phone and I'll take care of your hair,' Hilary suggested, planting herself between him and the door, relying on his essential male instinct to avoid acknowledging that he had made a mistake to guide him.

He flicked her a perplexed glance, the sort that told her he did not really see her and was much more interested in his phone conversation. She expected that to change when she wielded the styling scissors around him. In her admittedly slender experience handsome men were well aware of being handsome and as keen as any woman to ensure that their hair was cut only to their own exact specification.

'Do what needs to be done,' Roel told her impatiently.

Asked for guidance a second time, he gave her an

unbelieving appraisal. 'But it's only a haircut, nothing important.'

So she just copied the existing conservative style. Even the feel of his luxuriant black hair thrilled her fingertips. As he paid she urged him to make sure that he came back. He had just walked out when she noticed the large denomination banknote that she assumed he had accidentally dropped on the desk. Ever eager, she rushed out into the street after him.

'It's a tip,' Roel said in a pained tone when she attempted to return the money. He stared down at her from his great height while a limousine the length of a train drew up behind him and a uniformed chauffeur leapt out to throw open the passenger door for his entry.

'But it's too much…' she mumbled, staggered by the sight of that limo and the concept of a tip that size.

With a shrug of imperious dismissal, Roel swung away into his opulent car.

Hilary drifted back to the present to discover that while she had been lost in her thoughts Roel had contrived to regain his natural colour and was upright again.

'Should you be standing?' Hilary queried, watching him set down the phone he had been using.

'We're going home,' Roel imparted, ignoring the question.

In search of support, Hilary looked in dismay at the consultant. 'Dr Lerther?'

The older man aimed a stiff smile at her. 'There is no physical reason why your husband should remain at the clinic.'

'*Naturalmente…*the other problem will vanish,' Roel pronounced with supreme confidence.

We're going home. Home? For goodness' sake, where was home? Caught totally unprepared for the development, Hilary followed Roel out to the lift, which swept them down to the ground floor. There she learned that the case she had left at reception had already been stowed in the transport awaiting them.

'So where were you when I crashed my car yesterday?' Roel enquired a tinge drily.

'In London…er…I have a business there,' Hilary answered in an undertone while she frantically wondered what she was supposed to do or say next for she had no script on which to act. Nothing was as she had assumed it would be. He was walking wounded, conscious, but by no stretch of the imagination was he himself.

A limousine with tinted windows sat outside the clinic. A chauffeur doffed his cap. She climbed in and sank into a seat upholstered in rich hide leather. She struggled not to gawp at the astonishing luxury of the car interior.

'How long have we been married?' Roel drawled softly.

Without looking at him, Hilary breathed in deep. 'I think it'll be more relaxing if I don't force-feed you facts—'

Roel reached out a lean brown hand and closed long, sure fingers over hers. 'I want to know everything—'

Startled by the ease with which he had touched her, Hilary could not prevent her fingers from trembling within the hold of his. 'Dr Lerther said that telling you things that you didn't really need to know would just complicate matters—'

'Let me decide what I need to know,' Roel incised without hesitation.

'I think Dr Lerther has your best interests at heart and I don't want to risk your recovery by going against his advice,' Hilary confided unevenly, for that physically close to him for the first time ever she was a bundle of nerves.

'That's nonsense.'

'In a few days you'll have remembered it all for yourself,' Hilary pointed out in urgent consolation, appreciating how much more that scenario was likely to appeal to him. 'It would be better that way…much better.'

In her eagerness to convince him that patience was his best option, Hilary finally dared to glance up. She met his dark golden gaze in a head-on collision. Her mouth dried and her heart pounded like crazy.

'And in the short term?' Roel prompted in his dark, deep drawl.

His delicious growling accent seemed to shimmy down her sensitive spine and set up a chain reaction through her tense body. She was welded to the spot by the electrifying gold of his appraisal; her mind was a blank. 'The short term…?' she parroted like someone who had never heard the expression before.

'You and I,' Roel specified with a low-pitched laugh that sent the colour flying up into her cheeks while she stared up at him with eyes the same shade as winter skies. 'What do I do with a wife I've forgotten?'

'You don't need to do anything. You just trust her to l-look out for you,' Hilary stammered, fighting with every fibre of her being to suppress her embarrassing lack of self-control around him. Why was she hanging on his every word like a lovelorn schoolgirl and gaping at him like a star struck fan? She was infuriated by her own weakness. Her role was to be a supportive friend, nothing more, nothing less. But the sheer thrill level of just being alone with Roel seemed to have stolen her wits.

'Look out for me?' Roel studied her from below black spiky lashes. She was planning to look out for him? In all his life he did not think that he had ever heard anything more naive or ridiculous. Yet he said nothing because she shone with sincerity and good intentions.

'That's what I'm here for...' Hilary extended, but she could hardly find her voice to make that added assurance for her vocal cords were threatening to let her down. His proximity and the casual confidence with which he touched her were sending her brain into freefall.

Even as she spoke Roel raised a hand to let his forefinger trace the luscious fullness of her soft pink lower lip and that did nothing to cool her temperature. Indeed, where he touched her skin seemed to tighten with an awareness so acute it almost hurt to experience it. Leaning closer without even being aware of it, Hilary gave an almost imperceptible gasp as her nipples hardened into stiff straining points below her tee shirt.

'You're trembling...' Roel murmured huskily. 'But then why not? This is a stimulating situation.'

'I beg your pardon...?' Hilary whispered, convinced she had misheard him.

'A wife I've forgotten,' Roel quipped, watching her

with eyes as bright and tough as metallic bronze. 'A woman with whom I must have shared many intimacies but who appears to me at this moment in the guise of a complete stranger. It's a sexually intriguing concept, *cara mia*. How could it be anything else?'

CHAPTER THREE

A RIVER of bright guilty colour washed up Hilary's throat and surged as high as her hairline.

Sexually intriguing? Hilary shifted on her seat. *A woman with whom he had shared many intimacies?* Naturally Roel would make that assumption. It would not occur to him that she could be anything other than a normal wife. After all their arrangement nearly four years back had been highly unusual in its terms.

'You have a novel way of viewing things,' she muttered awkwardly, fighting not to betray how uncomfortable she was.

'You blush like an adolescent,' Roel noted with husky amusement.

'Absolutely *only* with you!' Hilary shot back at him, infuriated by the suspicion that her face was hot enough to fry eggs on. As a teenager her habit of flushing to the roots of her hair when she got embarrassed had made her the butt of many jokes at school. Mercifully she had grown out of the affliction but *not*, it seemed, around Roel.

'We can't have been married long,' Roel commented, his rich dark drawl roughening and slowing as he reached out and tugged her into his arms.

'Don't!' Hilary yelped as though he had pushed a panic button.

An involuntary grin crossed Roel's lean, darkly handsome face because, although she wasn't much bigger than a doll, she had an extremely bossy streak.

'Don't worry…kissing my wife is unlikely to put me back into hospital—'

'How do you know that?' Hilary demanded jerkily, angling her blonde head back a little more out of reach. Yet her every physical prompting urged her just to throw herself at him and make hay while the sun, as it were, shone. 'I just don't think there should be any kissing…yet—'

'*Non c'e problema,*' Roel teased, in his element, reading the look of concern that his wife wore and more amused than ever by her fear that sexual activity might somehow be detrimental to his health. 'Think of it as a useful experiment. It might even awaken lost memories, *bella mia.*'

'Roel…'

But anticipation was rising at wicked speed inside Hilary: she didn't want to stop him; she didn't have the will-power to stop him; she couldn't wait to experience what she had once been denied. And when his wide, sensual mouth tasted hers the pathways between every erogenous zone she possessed turned to liquid fire and blazed. Her heart thumped with mad, crazy excitement.

Long fingers sliding into her hair, he tilted her head back the better to gain access to her mouth. She leant back into the strong arm, bending her spine in the most encouraging way imaginable. He dipped his tongue between her readily parted lips and plundered the inner sweetness with a driving male hunger that took her by storm. Her body leapt into almost agonising life, pulses racing and nerve-endings quivering. Forbidden heat surged at the very heart of her. Defenceless against her own desire, she moaned low in her throat in response.

Dragging in a ragged breath of restraint, Roel released her. Ebony lashes veiling his gaze to a reserved flash of gold, he murmured without expression, 'We're home.'

Breathless and dazed by that unfamiliar explosion of passion, Hilary lowered her head and tried to get a grip on herself. Deep down inside her body in a private place that she wasn't even used to thinking about, she was conscious of a wicked ache of disappointment. She had got carried away: he could have made love to her on the back seat of his limo and he probably knew it. Hilary was so ashamed of herself for encouraging him that she wondered how she would ever look him in the face again. She had behaved like a sex-starved groupie let loose on her idol. What on earth was she playing at? He had accepted her on trust and, to be worthy of that trust, she needed to keep a proper distance between them! When the chauffeur opened the door beside her, she scrambled out of the limo in haste and only then took a good look at her surroundings.

Home? Roel appeared to live in a vast stone mansion set within the seclusion of high screening walls. A middle-aged manservant was stationed beside the imposing entrance. The huge hall was adorned with classical statues, gilded furniture and a marble floor. She was intimidated by such grandeur, and her steps faltered.

'*Santo cielo…*'

Roel's roughened exclamation made Hilary spin round. Wearing a stark frown of disconcertion, he seemed to be staring at the handsome marble fireplace. Swift understanding gripped her. Something had surprised Roel. Something was different or at

least not as he had expected. As he evidently had no
memory of the change taking place, he would naturally feel disorientated, and when that happened
within his own home it had to be that much more
disturbing.

Aware of the manservant's covert scrutiny, Hilary
hurried over to Roel, tucked a confiding hand into his
arm and stretched up to whisper, 'Let's go upstairs…'

In the very act of wondering why one of his grandfather's favourite paintings should be hanging in his
grandson's town house, Roel reacted to that breathy
little feminine invitation as red-blooded males had
done for centuries. The conundrum of the painting
momentarily forgotten, he was startled by a desire to
scoop his diminutive wife up and kiss her breathless
for reading his mind with such accuracy. Was that
how he usually acted around her? It shook him to
acknowledge that he had no idea.

'I just remembered something…you go on ahead,'
Hilary said when they reached the marble landing
above. Pulling free, she then hurried back downstairs
to speak to the manservant before he could disappear
from view.

'I'm sure you're wondering who I am,' Hilary began uncomfortably. 'You are…?'

'Umberto, *signorina*. I run the household and you
are Mr Sabatino's guest,' the older man responded
smoothly.

'I'm not…actually, I'm Roel's…er…wife, Hilary,'
she explained in an apologetic undertone.

Well-trained though Umberto was, he could not
conceal his surprise.

'Please ensure that no personal or business phone
calls are put through to my husband.'

Umberto stiffened, his lips parting in an anxious way.

'Don't ignore my instructions,' Hilary added, tilting her chin.

When she drew level with Roel again, he dealt her a keen appraisal and then, strong mouth quirking, he bent down and swept her up into his arms.

'Roel?' Hilary squawked, utterly taken aback by his behaviour. 'What on earth are you doing?'

Striding across the elegant landing, Roel vented a husky, sexy laugh and deftly shouldered open the door of the master bedroom suite. 'Ensuring that last-minute instructions to Umberto concerning dinner or whatever…won't interrupt us again!'

'Please put me down…' Hilary pressed in an enervated rush. 'You're supposed to be resting, Roel.'

Roel lowered her down onto a massive bed with exaggerated care. 'I have every intention of doing so…but only if I have company to do it with, *cara*.'

Hilary rolled over and off the other side of the bed. Her face was pink with embarrassment. 'That wouldn't be restful—'

Lean fingers jerked loose his silk tie, pulled it free and discarded it. Glinting golden eyes flared back at her in blatant challenge. 'I don't need to recall the last five years to know that I'm not a restful individual or given to lazing about doing nothing. If I'm not working, I require occupation—'

'But not this,' Hilary slotted in breathlessly. 'You only think that you want to sleep with me but you don't…not really, you don't. You just want to make me feel more familiar—'

'I can't believe I married a woman who makes a

three-act major production out of sex,' Roel incised
with biting derision.

'I'm trying to think of you, that's all.' Hilary
twisted her hands together in an unwittingly revealing
gesture of stress. 'This isn't what you need right
now—'

'Allow me to decide that.' But Roel had fallen still
and his brilliant eyes no longer appeared to be focused on her. His wide sensual mouth twisted and
then set into a grim line.

'What is it?' Hilary asked worriedly.

Roel glanced back at her, his stunning dark gaze
bleak and bitter, hard cheekbones prominent below
his olive skin. 'Clemente, my grandfather, is
dead...*that's* why the Matisse painting is here in our
home instead of at the *castello*. Am I right?'

As he spoke Hilary lost colour.

'On this score, you don't withhold information,'
Roel warned her icily.

Eyes stinging with tears of sympathy, Hilary nodded confirmation with pained reluctance. 'Yes, I'm
sorry. Your grandfather died four years ago—'

'How did he die?' Roel demanded.

'A heart attack. I believe it was very sudden,'
Hilary proffered, grateful that she at least knew that
much and praying that he would ask for no other details.

Roel swung away from her and strode over to the
tall windows. His powerful shoulders were rigid with
tension below the expensive cloth of his jacket. He
was closing her out and she knew it. He had mentally
dismissed her from his presence as surely as if he had
slammed a door in her face.

'Roel…' she murmured, aching with a compassion she was afraid to show for fear of offending.

'Go check the dinner menu,' he advised very drily.

Hilary's troubled gaze sparked and she stood taller. 'I couldn't care less about stuff like that. Don't push me away. I was very close to my gran and I was devastated when she passed away—'

'Some of us choose not to parade private emotions,' Roel whipped back.

'OK…OK!' Hilary threw up both hands in a peace-making gesture, expressive brows raised at his vehemence.

Face pale and tight with discomfiture, for he could not have rejected her attempt to offer comfort more clearly, she spun round and walked out of the room.

So what do you do for an encore? a snide little voice asked inside Roel's head. Kick puppies? Do a Scrooge for the festive season?

Umberto was in the corridor. With him was another man, who was carrying her case. Hilary came to an abrupt halt.

'*Signora.*' With a smooth inclination of his head, the manservant thrust open the door of the next room and stood back so that she could enter it first.

His and hers bedrooms, Hilary registered, blinking at the magnificence of the furniture and the awesome amount of space. Just as well it didn't seem to be the thing for wealthy husbands and wives to share the same room. My goodness, that could have got really embarrassing, she told herself. But that attempt to give her thoughts a different direction didn't work. Nor did pursing her lips so hard they went numb. When she got an unwelcome glimpse of her reflection in a fancy dressing mirror, she could see that her eyes were still overbright with the threat of stupid, weak, impressionable tears! How could one hard word from Roel turn her to weepy mush?

Why did she have to recall that Roel had once acted more relaxed around her? Yeah, much as if she were the equivalent of hair-trimming wallpaper, she jeered inwardly. But it was true. One day when she had confided how much she still missed her gran he had started telling her about how his grandfather, Clemente, had gone to Nepal to 'find himself' when he was sixty-five years old. Better late than never, she had teased and Roel had groaned.

Snatching in a stark breath, Hilary made herself concentrate and she followed Umberto from the room. 'I'd appreciate a quick tour of the house,' she told him with a friendly smile, knowing that the request was a necessity. She could hardly pretend that she had been living below Roel's roof if she didn't even know her way round it.

Even so the amount of deception involved in the pretence she had taken on with such little forethought was beginning to unnerve Hilary. In just a couple of days, she reflected, Roel would surely regain his memory and he would have no further need for her then. Would he appreciate that she had been trying to help him out? That in fact she had only acted like a good mate?

Umberto was very precise. He would have been happy to show her the interior of every cupboard. Hilary speeded h.m up by darting from one room to the next, amazed at the sheer size of the house, daunted by the extreme formality of the furniture and all the staff but enchanted by the many paintings. In the basement kitchen she made the acquaintance of

the chef but demonstrated dismay rather than appro-
bation when she learned that the exact same menus
were rotated on a seasonal basis every year. Scenting
the likelihood of greater gastronomic freedom, the
French chef kissed her hand, rushed out to the back
garden, plucked a vibrant yellow rosebud and raced
after her to bestow it on her. Laughing, she slid the
bloom into her hair and went back upstairs to freshen
up before dinner.

The slender contents of her suitcase had already
been tidied away into the dressing room. She had to
open every drawer and wardrobe door to find a
change of clothes. The shower in the *en suite* was a
multi-jet delight. Smiling at such unfamiliar luxury
and wrapped in a giant fleecy towel, she padded bare-
foot out of the bathroom again.

Roel was in the bedroom waiting for her. She
jerked to a halt, her bemused gaze taking in the open
door that evidently connected with his room.

'*Dio mio*…I like the rose,' Roel murmured softly.

Hilary semi-raised a self-conscious hand to the bud
that she had threaded back into her hair again. 'Your
chef gave it to me…'

Roel had shed his business suit for black designer
chinos of faultless cut and a blue casual shirt. He
looked so downright gorgeous that she couldn't stop
staring. His smouldering dark sexual attraction hit her
like a tidal wave and swept her straight out of her
depth and under.

Her admission made Roel quirk an ebony brow. He
was not amused by his chef's impertinence. Yet he
could see what had inspired the gesture. His wife had
flawless skin, grey eyes as deep as a northern glacier
lake and a mouth as provocatively ripe as a cherry.

He felt his body harden with almost scientific interest. Every time he saw her, did he always want to have her again? Was he always *this* hungry to sink into that slim, shapely body of hers?

The awareness of her own naked skin below the towel gripped Hilary with painful shyness. She was mortified by the generous swell of her full breasts above the fleecy fabric but when she collided with Roel's burning golden gaze her embarrassment was blotted out by the strength of her own response to his overwhelming masculinity. The tingle in her pelvis expanded into a burst of shameless heat and her legs shook. She couldn't move, couldn't even think of anything to say.

The atmosphere was electric.

'I want you, *cara*,' Roel breathed.

That confession sent pleasure and pain rushing through Hilary in equal parts. Once she had nurtured secret fantasies of such a magical moment. The moment when Roel would miraculously cast aside all formality and see her as a desirable woman. What had once been her most fervent dream was actually happening. Roel was saying he wanted her and in every one of her dreams she had always thrown herself at him in joyful reward. Only in the present circumstance that was not an indulgence that she could allow herself.

Roel didn't really want *her*, Hilary reminded herself with pained reluctance. He was expressing a natural desire for a woman who was in fact an illusion: his wife, the woman he believed he had a normal marriage with and whom he understandably believed he could trust. But she was not that mythical wife. She was just someone he had once paid to go through a wedding ceremony with him, someone whom he cared nothing about on a personal basis. And as if all that were not enough, she was also way beneath his touch in terms of status and success.

Interpreting the forlorn air of desperation that her expressive face wore, Roel was frowning with incomprehension when he reached for her. 'Hilary—?'

'We don't have this sort of relationship,' Hilary protested half under her breath.

Ignoring her evasive step back from him, Roel closed long fingers round her wrist to halt her steady retreat. 'I don't understand—'

Tears clogged her throat, for doing what she accepted was right was the hardest thing she had ever had to do in her life. 'Look, it's not important and certainly nothing for you to worry about. But just take it from me, I'm really not a big deal in your life and when you get your memory back you'll remember that and be glad I put you on your guard—'

Roel had stilled. Brilliant eyes shimmering down at her, his questioning gaze narrowed with suspicion. 'What have you done that I should treat you in such a way?'

Taken aback by his reaction, Hilary paled in consternation. 'I haven't *done* anything!'

Roel appeared to have forgotten his own strength, for his fierce grip was threatening to crush the narrow bones of her wrist and she was provoked into a gasp of discomfort. 'You're hurting me...'

Instantly he released her and his concern and his apology were immediate but his next words made it clear that the issue under discussion was not to be so easily set aside. 'Explain what you meant by describing yourself as not being a big deal in my life.'

'All I meant was that you're so busy working you hardly notice I'm around,' Hilary mumbled weakly.

'If you've been unfaithful don't make a mystery of it,' Roel drawled with stinging softness. 'Just pack and get out of my life again.'

Hilary realised that she had stirred up a hornet's nest. Instead of prompting Roel to exercise greater reserve around her she had made the mistake of rousing more stressful concerns. Dismayed, she spluttered, 'Don't be ridiculous…of course I haven't been unfaithful to you!'

'Sabatino men have a habit of marrying flighty women,' Roel derided with a brooding roughness of pitch that was entirely new to her, but which carried an impressive note of foreboding. 'But we waste no time in divorcing them.'

'I'll consider myself warned,' Hilary told him, striving in vain to come up with a light-hearted smile before she vanished back into the bathroom.

In bewilderment, Roel fell back a step. His keen mind was seething with fast and furious questions.

We don't have *this* sort of relationship.

I'm not a big deal in your life.

You're so busy working you hardly notice I'm around.

What kind of a marriage was it where, young though they both were, they were already occupying separate bedrooms? Had that been his choice? She had implied that their relationship was as *he* wanted it to be. He was angry at the conclusions he was being forced to draw. Failure was anathema to him. Instinct had always made him strive for perfection in every facet of his life. Yet it seemed his marriage was in trouble. Without any apparent desire to rebuke or challenge him, his wife had given him a picture of himself as a workaholic husband indifferent to her needs. He could barely bring himself to credit that he rarely slept with her either. But what else was he to think? Now he could look back and recognise that her initial response to being kissed in the limo had been shock and surprise. Shock and surprise followed by an undeniably eager and encouraging response, he reminded himself. So what was wrong could be fixed...*easily*!

Hilary got dressed. She put on a stretchy black skirt that ended four inches above the knee and teamed it with a fitted green top that had ribbon ties. Having checked the time, she called her sister's mobile phone.

'I've been thinking about you all day...how's Roel doing?' Emma demanded anxiously.

'Basically he's all right but that head injury is still causing him some problems. He's not quite himself yet.'

'Meaning?' her sister probed.

'That, right now, I can make myself useful over here...purely as a friend,' Hilary hastened to add.

Almost four years ago, she had not told her sister the truth about her marriage of convenience. She had been afraid that if she did Emma would lose respect both for her and for the institution of marriage. What had then seemed to be a harmless fib couched for the sensitive ears of a girl of thirteen, however, now seemed rather more dishonest and less forgivable. When the emergency with Roel was over, Hilary knew that it would only be fair if she told Emma the whole story. She wasn't looking forward to the challenge but she knew she could not allow the younger woman to go on believing that she herself might have contributed in some way to the demise of her big sister's marriage.

'Exactly what is wrong with him?'

Hilary took a deep breath and explained in a few words.

'You know what all this means?' Emma exclaimed. 'This is going to give you and Roel the chance to make a completely fresh start!'

'There's no question of anything like that.' Hilary sighed, her face clouding with unease. 'I just want to help him out…that's all.'

When she went downstairs, Umberto ushered her into the candle-lit dining room where the table glittered with crystal, gleaming china and heavy silver cutlery. Fresh lilies with petals as pale and perfect as snow ornamented the polished wood.

'This is just *so* beautiful,' Hilary was telling the older man when Roel entered.

Roel almost groaned out loud when he saw the embellished table arrangements. *Inferno!* What was the special occasion? Was it her birthday or their anniversary?

'Are we celebrating something?' he enquired.

Hilary went pink and picked up her glass of wine with a nervous hand. 'Your release from hospital, I expect.'

'I've come up with a safe conversational topic,' Roel informed her. 'Tell me about your family.'

Truth to tell, Hilary could not see a problem with discussing her own background with him. 'There's not much in the way of family to talk about—'

'Your parents?' Having repeated that demand for

information, Roel lounged back in his chair with a daunting air of expectancy.

'They're dead...in a car crash in France when I was sixteen,' Hilary explained heavily. 'My sister, Emma, was eleven.'

Roel frowned. 'Who took charge of you?'

'We lived with my father's cousin.' Hilary saw no reason to burden him with the reality of what an unhappy and short-lived arrangement that had turned out to be. 'Emma's at boarding-school now.'

'Here in Switzerland?'

Hilary stiffened. 'No. In England.'

'No other relatives?'

'None. My gran mostly raised me,' she volunteered. 'She was Italian and when I was a child she lived with us and that was how I communicated with her.'

'Yet you don't speak Italian now with me?' Roel censured in the same language but his incisive dark eyes were forgiving because she had established a link between their backgrounds that he respected.

She winced. 'No way. I understand much more than I can speak—'

'Time that that changed,' Roel decreed without hesitation.

'No.' Hilary continued to answer him in English, her chin at a stubborn angle, remembered humiliation in her gaze. 'You once laughed yourself sick at my Italian!' she condemned. 'You said I sounded like a hill-billy because some of the words I used were out of date.'

'I was teasing you, *cara*.' Amusement and satisfaction combined in Roel's response for she had forgotten her embargo on talking about the past.

Her face shadowed. No, he had not been teasing her; he had been annoyed with her for having sufficient grasp of Italian to follow what he had arrogantly deemed to be a confidential conversation. 'We had a bit of an argument,' she admitted stiffly, 'but I don't want to discuss it.'

It was better to stay silent than risk giving him the wrong impression, Hilary decided uneasily. She concentrated on eating instead and the food was delicious. Umberto refreshed her wineglass on at least three occasions. She refused coffee and announced that she was going to bed early because she was tired.

'It is barely eight o'clock,' Roel pointed out gently.

'I never stay up late,' Hilary told him woodenly and stood up.

Roel thrust back his chair and rose. As she passed by he closed a hand over hers. 'One question you *must* answer—'

'No...don't say that to me,' Hilary muttered in alarm.

Diamond-hard dark eyes sought hers and brooked no denial. 'Whose idea was it that we use separate bedrooms?'

Her mouth ran dry. 'Yours...' she told him, recognising that that was the only sensible reply that she could give.

A scorching smile slashed Roel's handsome mouth. Her heart hammered in response like a bird trapped inside a cage. He released his hold and she stepped back from him on knees that felt wobbly.

'Goodnight,' she muttered hurriedly and fled.

Ten minutes later, her teeth brushed and her face bare of cosmetics, she switched out the light and leapt into her comfortable bed with an appreciative sigh.

But her adrenalin was still on too high a charge to allow her to relax into sleep and her restless thoughts strayed back to the past and her initial meetings with Roel.

She had fallen in love with a guy who never even took her out on a date. About once a month he had returned to the salon where she worked. In the aftermath of his first visit, for his limo and the size of that tip had been noticed, the most senior stylist had insisted on taking Hilary's place. To Hilary's surprise and delight, Roel himself had objected to the change of personnel and had asked specifically for her.

'Did you remember my name?' Hilary questioned.

'I described you.'

'How?' she prompted with unhidden eagerness.

'Do you always talk this much?'

'If you tell me how you described me, I'll shut up,' she promised.

'Very small, purple lips, workman's boots.'

She was less than thrilled by that portrayal but after five minutes she forgot her promise to give him peace and soon became engaged in finding out what age he was and whether or not he was single. In the appointments that followed, it would have been an untruth to say that he chatted to her but he didn't object to her chatting to him. She tried to get to know him by letting him get to know her. She asked him what he did for a living.

'I work in a bank.' A long time afterwards, she quite accidentally noticed the Sabatino name heading an article in the business section of a Sunday newspaper. That article revealed that, far from merely working in a bank, Roel pretty much *owned* a bank.

The day she heard him lamenting his grandfather's

will and the potential loss of the family home he so clearly loved, she leapt into his dialogue on pure impulse and offered to become his 'fake' wife. Breaking off from his phone call, he surveyed her in disbelief.

'Well, why not?' she continued, face burning at her own nerve in making such a suggestion, but even so she was desperate to grab at the chance to do something for him. Something, *anything*, that would make him more liable to take notice of her and maybe even like her.

'I can think of a thousand reasons why not,' Roel fielded in an icy putdown.

'Probably because you're a very cautious guy and you complicate things,' she pointed out gently. 'But you have a simple problem. You need a fake wife so that you can hang onto your home and I would help out—'

'I refuse to discuss this with you. You eavesdropped on a personal conversation.'

'Maybe you should ask one of your friends to help you out and stop being so proud,' Hilary advised in addition.

'Where did you learn to speak Italian like a hillbilly?'

'Like a *what*? What's wrong with my Italian?' she flamed back at him, distracted as he had no doubt intended by the insult.

Roel started to laugh. 'You use archaic words and expressions—'

'Sometimes,' Hilary seethed, 'you're incredibly rude!'

'You interrupted a confidential dialogue and slung an outrageous proposition at me. What did you expect?'

'I was offering to *help* you—'

'Why? We're strangers,' Roel derided.

Cut to the bone, she just jerked her chin down in a nod and shrugged her stiff shoulders. 'Sorry I spoke—'

'Sulking is not attractive.'

Hilary perked up at amazing speed. 'What *do* you find attractive about me?' she pressed hopefully, less than subtle at the age of nineteen years.

'Nothing,' Roel imparted drily.

'Come on…you don't mean it…there's got to be something reasonable about some part of me,' she cajoled.

Watching him in the mirror, she saw him smile. That rare, wildly charismatic smile that made her palms damp and her tummy flip. But he still refused to be drawn. Three weeks later, he phoned her at work and asked her to meet him for lunch at a hotel.

'Business,' he specified lest she get the wrong idea.

'I'm not fussy,' she admitted cheerfully. 'Don't be surprised if I dress up.'

While Roel spelt out the terms of the marriage of convenience that she herself had originally suggested might meet his requirements, he was terrifyingly businesslike. He killed her appetite and she ate nothing. He said he would have to compensate her for doing him a favour. She said no, she didn't want to be paid and she meant it. Then he mentioned a sum of money that bereft her of breath.

'Think it over and we'll discuss it next time I see you—'

'Look, if I had wanted money, I wouldn't have offered to do this. It wouldn't be right to take money for going through a marriage ceremony. I mean, all you want to do is hang onto the home that's been in your family for generations and there's no way you should have to pay me or anyone else to do that!'

Roel dealt her a cool, measuring scrutiny. 'I have no wish to become too personal but you live on the poverty line and you have little hope of improving your own prospects—'

'That's a matter of opinion—'

'A financial injection would give you choices you've never had before. You could go back to school—'

Hilary gave him an aghast look. 'No, thanks. It was bad enough the first time round. I didn't just end up doing what I do, you know…I always wanted to be a hairdresser and I love it!'

'You should continue your education,' Roel completed as though she hadn't spoken. 'Expand your horizons. You should be more ambitious.'

'Would you go out with me if I went to college?' Hilary asked in sudden hope. 'I suppose you wouldn't want to wait that long.'

'Don't be flippant. I was merely trying to offer you some advice.'

'And tempt me with your money.'

And he had tempted her successfully because in the days that followed she worked out that she could turn her life and her sister's life around with just a fraction of the vast sum of cash he had mentioned. If she found them a flat in a nicer area, she would be able to separate her sibling from the bunch of troublemakers that the younger girl was hanging around with. If she opened up a small hair salon of her own, she would be able to choose her own working hours and spend more time at home with Emma. In the end she agreed to accept a tithe of the amount he had wanted to give her. She was seduced by the idea of what she could do with that money and only after she accepted Roel's cheque did she realise how much of his respect she had lost.

As she suppressed a sigh for a past that could not be altered Hilary's mind roved back to the present. She was rudely sprung from her drowsiness by the sound of a door opening. A second later, lights illuminated the room. Startled and blinking furiously, she focused on Roel and tried to persuade her brain back into activity.

Before she could achieve that goal, however, an imperious hand closed over the edge of the bedding and flung it back from her prone body. She let out a yelp of mingled astonishment and mortification. He bent down and scooped her up like a parcel he had come to retrieve.

'What are you doing?' she squealed.

'From now on, we share the same bed, *cara*,' Roel delivered, striding back into his own room with both arms firmly wrapped round her.

'I don't think that's a good idea,' Hilary mumbled.

CHAPTER FOUR

ROEL settled Hilary down on his bed.

Feverish heat lit her cheeks. The short blue night-dress she wore had not been chosen for modesty. In the privacy of her own bedroom, Hilary loved to wear highly feminine lingeɪe that made her feel glamorous but she had never had an audience before. Thrusting herself up into sitting position, she yanked in desperation at the sheet, keen to cover her bare legs.

He unbuttoned his shirt and embarked on removing his shoes. She stopped breathing. She told herself to look away but she knew she wouldn't. She was twenty-three years old and she had never seen a man undress. She had never even been alone in a bedroom with a man. Why? She was still a virgin. In many ways she thought that she was still a virgin because she had met Roel first and learnt to want what she could not have.

At nineteen she had discovered that physical desire could cut like a knife through every thought and all pride. Roel might not have reacted to her in the same way but she had never forgotten the sheer exhilarating strength of her response to him. Every guy who came into her life after him had been measured up against the same yardstick. She had wanted to feel again what she had felt for Roel and it had made her picky.

'I'm going for a shower, *bella mia*…'

Face hot, she dredged her attention from the vibrant slice of muscular brown chest showing between the parted edges of his shirt. 'I'm not beautiful…don't call me that,' she muttered.

Roel came down on the bed on one knee. Laughing dark golden eyes assailed hers. 'If I tell you that you're beautiful, I mean it—'

'But—'

'You have a heavenly shape—'

'I'm not very tall—'

'But what there is of you is of exceptional quality. I keep on getting an irresistible urge to snatch you off your feet and flatten you to the nearest bed…so here you are.'

Roel vaulted off the bed and unzipped his well-cut trousers.

'You're supposed to be resting…' Hilary fought a valiant battle with her conscience and averted her eyes in chagrin at her own longing to spy on his every move. 'I should be in my own room.'

'Go to sleep and stop fussing.' Roel laughed.

He was laughing, smiling. He seemed happy in a way that was unfamiliar to her. She turned over and told herself that there was no harm in sharing the same bed. It was a gigantic bed. It would be silly of her to make a fuss about such a small thing. But suppose he rolled over in the middle of the night and…and became amorous. Yes, just suppose. Would she be able to resist him? She knew she wouldn't want to. Tears of self-loathing stung her eyes and she blinked them back furiously.

On the other hand, another inner voice reasoned, he would soon get his memory back and if something physical had happened between them before that point, how would he feel about it? He was a sophisticated single guy and sex was unlikely to be something he regarded in a serious way. If she acted casual, he would think it had not meant anything more to her. Hilary pressed cool fingers of restraint hard to her hot cheeks and strove to kill her own seditious thoughts stone-dead. She was mortified to appreciate that she was trying to talk herself into the conviction that it would be all right to let Roel do whatever he wanted to do with her.

'Still awake, *cara*?'

At the sound of his deep, dark drawl Hilary pulled her head out from under the pillow and peered at him over the top of the sheet.

Only a towel knotted round his sleek brown midriff, crystalline drops of water still glittering in the cluster of dark curling hair hazing his powerful pectoral muscles, Roel studied her with slumberous cool. Slowly she nodded. He sank down on her side of the bed and her heart started thumping so hard she thought she might be about to suffer a panic attack. He eased back the sheet degree by degree while she held her breath.

'I want to see you,' he told her almost roughly.

Her mouth tingled at the mere thought of his on hers.

'I want to see *all* of you…' he completed huskily.

She was going to say no, she really was just a whisper's breadth from mustering all her defences and saying no to herself and then disaster occurred: she met smouldering dark golden eyes and her conscience drowned there. 'Roel…'

'I like the way you say my name.' He leant down and tasted her pink mouth with devastating expertise. His tongue pried apart her lips. He delved deep and sure in an exploratory foray. As she made a low sound of driven response her hands flew up to sink into his luxuriant hair and hold him close.

'You have the most incredible mouth,' he growled, hauling her up into his arms and across his spread thighs.

Dazed grey eyes roved up to his darkly handsome features. 'We can't do this…' she warned him shakily. 'We just can't.'

'Watch me…' Roel invited thickly, deft fingers releasing the tiny provocative pearl buttons on the bodice of her nightdress.

He thrust back the fabric to expose her full breasts. '*Santo cielo*…you're gorgeous…'

She was blushing fierily. He toyed with the straining raspberry pink crests that crowned the ripe mounds. Her heart was racing so fast it felt as if it were in her throat. All at one and the same time she was shy and embarrassed and thrilled by his touch. With a groan of appreciation he lowered his proud dark head and captured a taut nipple with his mouth, teasing the tender bud with his teeth and his tongue.

'Oh…' Sensual shock engulfed her unprepared body. As a delicious sensation of pleasure-pain darted from the sensitive tip of her breast to the secret place between her thighs she jerked and dragged in an audible breath. Her neck extended and her head stretched back over his arm in surrender.

'Ever since I laid eyes on you at the clinic I've been thinking about spreading you across my bed. Instant lust,' Roel confided, spectacular golden eyes raking over her with raw masculine heat. 'Was it like that the first time I saw you?'

'You never said,' she muttered, pushing her face into his shoulder and hiding it there.

'So I don't share my every waking thought with you?'

'No…'

He pushed her back onto the pillows so that he could study her and he kissed her again long and hard. The kernel of heat in the pit of her tummy swelled and made her hips shift restively against the mattress.

'You're hot for me, *bella mia*,' Roel pronounced with satisfaction.

There was no denying that. Her body felt tight and tense and terrifyingly sensitive on the outside. She had never felt more aware of it. She had never, ever felt anything as strongly as the sensations he was introducing her to and that very intensity was the most complete seduction. She couldn't think, she could only feel. Burning with a dulled frustrating ache, she reached up to him with a need she could not control.

'Don't be in such a hurry,' he teased in a sexy undertone and he skimmed sure hands down over her hips to remove her nightdress. Hungry golden eyes scanned her ripe curves and centred on the tangle of silvery blonde curls at the apex of her thighs.

'Roel…' Hilary gasped for she was too conscious of her own imperfections to withstand that audacious appraisal, and with a stifled moan of embarrassment she rolled over and dragged the sheet over herself.

Vaulting upright, he shed the damp towel and her eyes flew wide and her mouth ran dry for he was boldly aroused. He also had the lithe sun-darkened magnificence and sleek muscular power of a born athlete. Unconcerned by his nudity, he padded back to the bed to join her. Anticipation gripped her like a shower of sparks lighting her up from within but she still couldn't meet his smouldering gaze.

'I want you,' he growled, repossessing her swollen mouth with the driving demand of his own. The erotic invasion of his tongue left her weak, submissive to the storm of his hot sexuality. 'But I also want to torment you with pleasure…'

She rejoiced in the weight of his hard naked body against her, linked her arms round his neck when he crushed her softer curves beneath his powerful torso. She couldn't get enough of his devastating mouth. Every kiss was in itself even more than she had once dreamt of and she was lost in a dark world of sensuality that was utterly new to her. She breathed in short little gasps. The expert attention he paid to her tender-tipped breasts was almost more stimulating than she could bear for she twisted and turned, little cries breaking low in her throat.

'I like watching you,' Roel confided.

The tight sensation of aching fullness between her thighs made her squirm. He touched her where she had never been touched before. He discovered the moist secret heart of her, traced the swollen entrance, forcing a pleading moan from her parted lips. She was on fire for him and writhing, enslaved by the fierce hunger he had unleashed in her.

'Roel…please,' she sobbed.

He drove her wild. In the grip of that fevered seduction, she was helpless and out of control. Waves of throbbing heat were washing over her. He tipped her back and plunged into her slick, damp core.

'You're so tight, *cara mia*,' he groaned with ragged pleasure while she was still in shock from that unfamiliar invasion.

He thrust again, overcoming her resisting flesh and

driving home to the very centre of her. She cried out in pain, startled tears pooling in her eyes.

Stilling, Roel stared down at her with incredulous force. 'You were still a virgin...or am I imagining things?'

Already her body was adjusting to the bold incursion of his and the sharp edge of pain had faded. Emotions and responses running at storm-force strength, she stretched up to give him a forgiving kiss. That Roel should be her first lover was what she had always dreamt of and she had no room for regret. 'I didn't know I could feel like this...don't stop—'

'My wife...a twenty-two-carat virgin,' Roel commented again, rich dark accented drawl not quite level.

Hilary wrapped her arms round him and angled up to him in frantic invitation. 'Please...'

As she made that instinctive movement of encouragement he succumbed and sank into her again. The racing excitement that had momentarily gone into abeyance claimed her afresh. With every fluid shift of his powerful body he mastered her and she surrendered to his primal rhythm with helpless abandon. The excitement built and built until she could have screamed with frustration and only then did he send her spiralling out of control into a convulsive climax of explosive pleasure. Bereft of all breath and voice in the aftermath of that revelation, she fell back against the pillows and lay shell-shocked for long moments afterwards.

Roel had made love to her and it had transcended her every naive expectation. However, not only was she already becoming guiltily, uneasily aware that she should not have succumbed to temptation, it was also dawning on her that in becoming intimate with Roel she had trapped herself into a tight corner. She had been too inexperienced to appreciate that Roel might realise that he was the very first lover she had ever had. She was supposed to be a married woman, not a virgin.

At that precise moment, Roel released her from his weight and curved a strong arm round her to carry her over into a cooler patch in the bed. Tawny eyes framed by dense black lashes inspected her hectically flushed face. He dropped a kiss on her brow. 'So…amazing virginal wife…is it possible that you are still almost a bride?'

Hilary paled and lowered her head. Of course he was now wondering if they were a newly married couple. If he had not been holding onto her, she would have taken refuge under the bed and refused to come out again. She was so ashamed of herself that she couldn't look at him and even less did she want to examine her own behaviour. Had she gone clean crazy?

'You're very quiet…' Roel remarked.

'Gosh, I'm dying for a shower!' Hilary exclaimed and practically threw herself out of the bed.

Escape having been the only thing on her mind, she was then aghast to appreciate that she was naked as the day she was born. Flopping down on her knees on the floor with more haste than grace, she scrabbled madly round the side of the bed to find her nightdress and put it on again with frantic hands. Decently covered again, cheeks fiery red, she endeavoured to stand up again and vacate the room in a more normal way.

Lounging back against the tumbled white pillows, Roel was frowning at her with complete incomprehension. *'Che cosa hai?'* he asked incredulously. 'What's the matter with you?'

Hilary forced a smile and aimed it in his general direction. 'What the heck could be the matter?' she fielded and, backing into her own bedroom, took to her heels the minute she knew she was out of view to lock herself into the adjoining bathroom.

What was Roel going to think of her when he recovered his memory? Fierce shame assailed her. He was going to think she was a pretty sad individual to have slept with him in such circumstances. Or was he more likely to recognise that only a truly besotted woman would have seized on the one chance she had had to get close to him? He would guess that she had fallen head over heels in love with him almost four years ago and still found him absolutely irresistible and he would think that she was totally pathetic. She cringed and died a thousand mental deaths at that threat.

In the bedroom next door the internal household phone buzzed and Roel answered it. Umberto informed him in an almost covert tone that a visitor had arrived.

'Who?' Roel queried even as he began to reach for his clothes.

The older man demonstrated a great reluctance to name the arrival but managed to get over the concept that that identity was a matter of immense necessary confidentiality.

Minutes later, Roel descended the stairs. 'Why all the mystery?' he asked his manservant, his tone dry in the extreme.

'The lady is Celine Duroux.'

Roel's strong facial bones clenched, for the name

meant nothing to him and he was infuriated and frustrated by that reality.

'Did I do wrong in allowing her into the house?' Umberto quavered.

Rebelling against the galling sense of being at a loss, which his amnesia had induced, Roel refused to lower himself to the level of taking the older man into his confidence. He would very much have liked to know why his employee should believe that the woman might reasonably have been refused entrance to his home. But ferocious pride kept Roel silent.

He entered the rarely used rear reception room where Umberto had stashed the unexpected guest. A beautiful green-eyed brunette surged towards him. Almost six feet in height with perfect features and the chic of a fashion model, she threw herself into his arms exclaiming, 'Have you any idea how frantic I've been? When you didn't show up yesterday, I simply assumed you were too busy. But when I heard a rumour that there'd been an accident, I just *had* to come here!'

Disconcerted by the intimacy of her greeting, Roel set her back from him. His piercing dark eyes were glacier-cool with caution.

'As you can see, your concern was unnecessary. I am in good health.'

Celine Duroux gave an exaggerated shiver. 'Don't be so cold with me,' she complained.

'Am I being cold?' Roel was playing for time.

The brunette pouted and sent him a provocative look through her eyelashes. The calculated artificiality that seemed to accompany her every word and gesture grated on him.

'OK…' she sighed. 'I know I shouldn't have come

here because you think your mistress should be ultra-ultra discreet. But it isn't the nineteenth century any more.'

Not by so much as a flicker of expression did Roel reveal the shock she had just dealt him. A four-letter exclamation that was a curse and a word he never utilised lit up like neon inside his brain. Finally he understood what had rocked Umberto's fabled nerves of steel. Celine Duroux was his mistress and sufficiently confident to visit his home even though she had to be aware that he was a married man.

Unhappily his mistress's attitude said a lot about what had to have been his own attitude towards his wife. It crossed Roel's mind that that four-letter word he had mentally applied to the situation might also be reasonably applied to his own character prior to the car crash. It did not take great genius to work out why his marriage appeared to have been under strain or why his wife had informed him that he paid her little attention: he was having an affair.

'I still think that it would have been wiser if you had resisted the urge to call here,' Roel countered. 'As you have, however, it's only fair to tell you that I believe our relationship has run its course and must now end.'

While Celine surveyed him in angry surprise, Roel concluded that speech with conventional regrets. He knew he did not sound convincing, but then his sole motivation at that point was to get Celine out of the house before Hilary was slapped in the face by the sight of her. He was not accustomed to finding himself in the wrong and he was furious at the revelation that his personal life was a mess. Celine had referred to his failure to show up for an appointment with her only yesterday. So, there was no doubt about it: he had been unfaithful to his wife. No wonder he had sensed so much tension in their relationship!

Did Hilary know about Celine? Of course she knew there was another woman! That had to be why their marriage had not been consummated. Had Hilary refused to sleep with him while he was still keeping a mistress? Doubtless warned by Dr Lerther not to give her husband any disturbing information, Hilary had told him nothing that might trouble him. Had it not been for her inability to hide her distress and confusion after they had shared a bed, he would undoubtedly have concluded that she was still a virgin only because they were newly married.

Instead he had been confronted by a far less pleasant explanation and guilt was a new experience for Roel. In fact as a Sabatino male he was used to holding the moral high ground. Sabatino men prided themselves on their sense of honour. It was their undeserving wives who had in recent generations proven their unworthiness with greed, promiscuity and moral weakness. But Hilary already seemed rather an improvement on the women chosen by his forebears, he acknowledged, his wide sensual mouth compressing.

He remained silent while Celine endeavoured to tease him into changing his mind before sharply accusing him of being cruelly insensitive. He said nothing. She would be richly compensated for the sudden termination of their arrangement. Without his encouragement the scene could not escalate and, outraged by her failure to have a discernible effect on him, Celine finally stalked past him and out into the hall.

Having gathered her courage to go off in search of Roel because she was worried that he had vanished from his bedroom when everything she had ever heard about men had led her to expect him to fall asleep after sex, Hilary was just in time to see Celine Duroux crossing the hall below. Hilary fell still on the upper landing and stared at the stranger with her tumbling mane of chestnut hair, dazzlingly lovely face and legs that looked as long to Hilary as her own entire body.

She watched the brunette depart and wondered who on earth she was. Had she been visiting Roel? Could she have been a girlfriend? For goodness' sake, why had it not occurred to her that Roel might be involved with someone? Overtaken by anxiety and unease, she hurried back to her own room and went to bed. Her last waking thought before exhaustion claimed her was that if Roel had had another woman in his life, his aunt would scarcely have contacted her in London.

Ten minutes later, Roel gazed down at his sleeping wife. Her lashes were clogged together as though she had been crying. The conscience he had not known he had until that moment slashed at him. He was such a bastard. There was nothing new in his awareness of that fact. Even as a teenager he had not wasted much time or thought on women. He had never loved and he had always left them. But *this* woman was in a class of her own because he had married her and made her unhappy. Her bitten nails spoke for her and she deserved better. She had not mentioned Celine. That was sensible; he would not raise that issue either. Some things were better left buried. In any case, as of tonight his wife was very much his wife and they would proceed from that point…

As Hilary wakened she stretched and the unfamiliar intimate ache between her thighs shot her back to full awareness faster than anything else could have done.

She looked at her watch in dismay for it was afternoon. Uneasy dreams had given her a disturbed night and she had slept late. Scrambling out of bed, she flung herself into the activity of getting up but all the time her mind was betraying her. She was remembering how Roel had looked while he was making love to her: his black hair damp, beautiful dark knowing eyes savage in their intensity. She quivered. Just thinking about Roel made her go weak at the knees. His outer shield of ruthless cool concealed a hot and passionate temperament.

But her biggest thrill had been the simple joy of being able to pretend that Roel was *her* guy. Ridiculous as it was, that had been her dream come true. The night before she had been overwhelmed by guilt at having slept with Roel. She had always been a very honest and straightforward person. Unfortunately circumstances had made it impossible for her to be honest with Roel. But now as she flung back the curtains on the clear bright light of day she decided that she had been over-tired and too hard on herself.

So…she had made love with Roel. While that had been a very big deal on her terms she doubted very much that he attached similar importance to the act of sex. He was very rich and very good-looking and whether she liked it or not he had to be very experienced with women. She might be his wife but he had had no memory of her whatsoever. Yet he had still taken her into his bed and had wasted no time in satisfying his high sex drive with her. To be frank, though, she had no complaints on that score. In fact, she reflected with guilty amusement, she might even be at risk of fawning on him like a willing slave girl in the hope that he would feel free to repeat what for her had been an extraordinarily pleasurable event.

Did she have the soul of a slut? No, she was still madly in love with him and she could not imagine ever sharing something so personal and intimate with anyone other than Roel. Why shouldn't she build up a few harmless memories for the future? Long after he had again forgotten that she even existed, she would be living alone and sleeping alone because she would always prefer that to settling for second-best. And next to Roel, who was fiercely handsome and sexy, not to mention intelligent and strong, other men just shrank in stature. That was why she had never managed to fall back out of love again. A sound came from the bedroom and she turned away from the bathroom vanity with a lipstick still clutched in her hand.

'Oh…it's you,' she muttered unsteadily when she saw her husband lodged in the doorway.

'*Dormiglione*…sleepy-head,' Roel said huskily.

Her attention glued to his lean powerful face and her heartbeat went haywire.

'You don't need this stuff.' Roel bestowed a frowning look of reproof on the sizeable collection of cosmetics scattered on the counter. 'Get rid of it.'

His domineering streak had come to her rescue. Turning back to the mirror, Hilary tilted back her head to paint her lips with a defiant hand. 'I like make-up.'

'But you must know that I don't,' Roel informed her in a tone that hinted at his amazement that she should be wielding a cosmetic wand in his vicinity.

'Well, it's good that you have a free choice *not* to wear make-up,' she pointed out.

'Don't be facetious. I dislike anything false.'

Hilary glossed her lips with a raspberry tint and gave him a forgiving grin. 'You're an amazing guy…you're just so controlling and spoilt—'

'Spoilt?' Roel repeated with an edge of disconcerted rawness.

'Every place you go you're surrounded by people you can order around. Servants, employees. I should think you'd get tired of being incredibly bossy but instead you seem to thrive on handing out orders—'

'Expressing a preference is not handing out an order,' Roel delivered icily.

'When you express a preference, it's the same thing as a command. But I'm not going to bin all my make-up just because you don't approve of it. You're wearing a pretty boring suit…are you about to throw it away because I think it's deeply untrendy?'

'I don't do trendy at the bank,' Roel told her drily.

'But you're not at the bank now,' she heard herself say, her voice husky from lack of oxygen and the disturbing little bubble of excitement flaring up inside her.

Without warning Roel snaked out his hands and caught her to him. 'You're very…feisty—'

With every sense leaping with wicked anticipation, Hilary sparkled up at him. He dragged her even closer. Adoring his hard, muscular strength, she melted into his overwhelmingly masculine frame. 'You mean cheeky?' she whispered.

Roel raised lean brown hands to her face and framed her cheekbones. Her grey eyes were mirrored pools of encouragement. His scorching golden gaze locked to her triangular features with hungry force. 'All I know is that you make me hot for you. If the maids weren't next door packing for you, I would take you up against the wall. I'd like to do it hard and fast and I think you'd like it too, *bella mia*.'

A wave of burning heat rose up under Hilary's skin in the mother of all blushes. She could barely credit that he had said such a thing to her but the sensual intensity of his appraisal underscored how serious he was. Her legs trembled. She felt wildly out of her depth but feverishly excited by his boldness. Her nipples had swollen into stiff peaks below her tee shirt and the forbidden tingle in her pelvis made her feel unbearably weak.

'And I believe I could do it without messing your make-up,' Roel continued in the same considering tone.

'Probably...' Her voice emerged a little squeakily.

Looked down at her passion-glazed face, Roel laughed with very male satisfaction. 'But I think I'll resist the urge until you take it off again!'

'You'll be waiting a very long time!' Mortified by his mockery, Hilary yanked herself back from him and then hesitated. Whether she wanted to or not, she knew that she really ought to ask him who his female visitor the night before had been. 'I saw the woman who called here to see you last night and I wondered who she was...'

As Roel stilled his stunning eyes veiled. 'What woman?'

Hilary reddened. 'She had long dark hair...she was very attractive...'

'Oh, that one...' Roel shrugged with magnificent

cool, not a muscle moving on his lean, intelligent face. 'She works for me.'

The current of relief that passed through Hilary left her feeling a little light-headed. It had been silly of her to take fright at the sight of the beautiful brunette. She heard someone in the bedroom next door ask Roel a question.

'Hilary?' Roel requested her attention. 'The maids say they can only find a handful of garments. Where is the rest of your wardrobe?'

Wrenched from abstraction with a vengeance, Hilary froze in strong dismay. Naturally Roel would expect her to have an extensive collection of clothes. Weren't all rich men's wives supposed to be mad about fashion? That dressing room ought to be lined with wall-to-wall designer stuff. How on earth was she to explain all those empty cupboards and drawers?

Frantically striving to come up with a good reason for her lack of clothing, Hilary drew level with Roel and shrugged. 'I decided to have a good old clean out,' she announced.

His ebony brows pleated. 'But according to our staff you have only two outfits here, *cara*.'

Hilary worried at her lower lip with her teeth and dropped her eyes. Her mind was a total blank. 'I got a bit carried away…?'

The silence stretched and she threw a nervous glance in his direction.

His lean, darkly handsome features were unreadable. He looked levelly back at her.

'I really must go shopping,' she mumbled.

'If I didn't know better, I would think you had been living somewhere else,' Roel commented.

'For goodness' sake…' Hilary exclaimed tautly.

'So explain the empty closets in a way I can believe.'

Taut as a bowstring, Hilary breathed in deep and, mercifully, inspiration grabbed her. 'We had a stupid row because you don't like my taste in clothes…and I was so annoyed with you, I dumped them all!'

Roel treated her to an appreciative appraisal. 'Now that, with your quick temper, I *can* picture.'

Some of her fierce tension ebbed. 'Why are the maids packing for me? Are we going somewhere?'

'The Castello Sabatino.'

CHAPTER FIVE

THE Castello Sabatino was a medieval castle that stood guard over a remote wooded valley that lay close to the Italian border. A still lake of crystal-clear water lapped the foot of the massive stone walls, acting like a mirror for the bright blue vault of the sky and the snow-capped majesty of the alpine peaks. Both the setting and the building were breathtakingly beautiful and Hilary was not at all surprised that Roel had been prepared to marry her to ensure that he kept his ancestral home.

The helicopter that they had boarded in Geneva landed on a purpose-built heli-pad. Having lifted her out with easy strength, Roel engulfed her hand in his to walk the last few yards. She watched him frowning into the sun and lowering his proud dark head as though the bright light were a knife.

'Are you feeling all right?' she asked worriedly.

'I'm a little tired, nothing more.' His dark, deep drawl was brusque, dismissive and laced with all the annoyance of a male unaccustomed to anything less than a full quota of buoyant energy. 'I went into my office at five this morning—'

Hilary stopped dead. 'You did…*what*?'

'I *am* the Sabatino Bank. It cannot easily manage without me,' Roel countered drily. 'I had to familiarise myself with current events, ensure that business could continue without me and deal with what I did not understand.'

'I can't believe that less than twenty-four hours after your doctor told you to rest you went into that
wretched bank at the crack of dawn!' Hilary fired at
him in shaken reproof.

'I did what had to be done.'

She studied his hard jaw line. It might as well have
been etched in stone. He was so stubborn she could
have screamed. In the unforgiving strong light his olive complexion had an ashen quality. He looked exhausted.

'You really don't have any respect for your own
health.'

As Roel strode beneath the ancient arched entrance
to the Castello Sabatino he shot her a hard-edged impatient glance. 'Did you imagine that I could simply
stage a vanishing act? Were I to absent myself from
the bank without an explanation, it could cause a
panic that would ultimately damage business.'

'So what was your explanation?' Hilary prompted,
watching what she was quite certain were lines of
pain settle between his pleated ebony brows.

'I said that the impact of the accident had left me
suffering from double vision and that I must rest my
eyesight. In that way I was able to access useful information from my executive assistants without cre-
ating comment.'

'Really, really sneaky,' Hilary conceded in grudging admiration.

'I added that I would take advantage of the en-
forced break from work to enjoy a vacation with my
wife.'

'My goodness…were people surprised?' Hilary
asked, dry-mouthed, for Umberto's dumbfounded response to the news that Roel had a wife had given

her the impression that with the exception of his aunt, Bautista, he had indeed kept their marriage a closely guarded secret. So any seemingly casual reference to his suddenly having acquired a wife would certainly have startled his staff at the bank.

'Their surprise was understandable,' Roel fielded. 'I am not in the habit of taking time off. By the way, you should have discussed barring all my phone calls with me.'

Hilary went pink. 'You would've insisted that you could handle them.'

'In the short term, it was good thinking.' Acknowledging the respectful greeting of a middle-aged housekeeper whom he addressed as Florenza, Roel stilled at the foot of a mellow stone staircase. 'But don't take action again on my behalf *without* prior consultation,' he concluded with measured censure.

Stung by that reproof, Hilary opened her mouth on heated words.

Roel pressed a taunting forefinger against her parted lips and she shivered, suddenly achingly conscious of the size and power of his lean, hard physique that close to her own. 'You know I'm right—'

'No, I *don't* know that you're right...what's wrong?'

Roel was staring down at her with brooding concentration. For perhaps a tenth of a second, his lush black lashes swept down and he frowned before lifting them again to focus on her with dazed and questioning force. 'You ran out into the street after me...'

In the wake of that strange statement, Hilary regarded him with incomprehension. But when he pressed an uncertain hand to his damp brow, she reacted. 'Roel? For goodness' sake, come and sit down—'

'No…' Roel incised almost roughly and he closed an imprisoning arm round her narrow waist instead. 'We'll go upstairs and talk about this in private.'

'Talk about what?' she whispered, her nerves leaping about like jumping beans.

And then the proverbial coin dropped and she understood: *you ran out into the street after me.*

'You've just remembered something from the past…' Hilary framed, her tummy lurching with fierce tension. 'And you've remembered something about me…'

'It was as though someone had flashed an old photograph in front of me…' In an impatient movement, Roel thrust open a door into an elegant reception room. Although that brief flare of lost recollection had disconcerted him, he had gained visible strength from it. 'You were trying to return the tip I'd left…'

'Yeah…' Her hands wound together and then parted and then laced back together again to flex.

Roel gazed at her in bewildered disbelief. 'Why would I have been tipping you? Was that a joke or something?'

Hilary turned pale as death and hurt as much as if he had slapped her. She could already see the chasm opening up between them. She was not what he had expected her to be. She was not and could never be a part of his privileged world. 'I'd just cut your hair…'

'My hair?' Roel stared at her much as if she had suddenly started performing back flips for his amusement.

Hilary compressed her lips and gave a tight nod of

confirmation. 'I'm…I'm a hairdresser. That business with the tip you left happened the very first time we met—'

'*Inferno!* I can recall everything I was feeling and thinking in that one tiny moment in the street! You had me as hard as a rock,' Roel admitted with shattering frankness, his fierce gaze wholly pinned to her. 'I wanted to haul you into the limo, check into a hotel and have a lost weekend.'

Hot pink flooded her triangular face and then slowly and painfully receded again. Well, at least he wasn't throwing her any false sentimental lines. She should be grateful to learn that he had found her attractive even though he had been far too aloof to show the fact. But she wasn't grateful. She was hurt and furious. A lost weekend? Was that all she had seemed good for? A right little tart likely to go to a hotel with a guy she barely knew for casual sex? Anguish arrested her feverish thoughts at that point. She would have gone. Maybe not that first day but later, if he had asked, she would have gone because by that stage she had been so besotted she would have settled for anything she could get. Even if that did encompass just the physical side of things, she conceded, her throat closing over with angry tears.

'*Scusate!* I should not have said that.' Roel lounged back against the wall, visibly struggling to master the total exhaustion weighting him.

'Oh, don't let it worry you. I'm not thin-skinned,' Hilary told him in an artificially bright voice. 'Please lie down for a while. You look ill.'

Shedding his tie and unbuttoning his shirt where he stood, he strode heavily through to the connecting bedroom.

'I think I should call the doctor,' Hilary remarked from the doorway.

'*Dannazione*…there's nothing the matter with me!' Roel slashed back at the speed of a cracking whiplash. 'Stop fussing.'

Hilary watched him sink down onto the bed and then tumble back against the pillows. He had not even removed his shoes. She pulled the blinds at the windows. Eyes semi-closed, he extended a lean hand in a graceful conciliatory gesture.

'You should know by now that I make my own decisions, *cara mia*.'

'That's not a problem,' Hilary assured him tenderly, strolling back and sitting down on the bed to let her small fingers curl into the warm clasp of his. No, his desire to make his own decisions was not a problem as long as his decisions agreed with her own conclusions.

'What I said…that flash of memory caught me off guard and I was crude.'

'Not crude,' Hilary responded in a quiet voice as sweet as honey, for she was determined to get her own back for the hurt he had caused her. 'A bit basic, but I can forgive you this once because the rest of the time you are the most romantic guy I've ever known.'

Roel's grip on her hand loosened and his spiky black lashes lifted on stunned dark golden eyes. 'Romantic…?' he parroted.

Even in the shattered state he was in, his wide sensual mouth was ready to curl with extreme scorn at such a suggestion. 'You're teasing me…'

'No, I'm not,' Hilary asserted.

Roel tugged her below a powerful arm and muttered sleepily. 'You can stay until I fall asleep.'

She almost made the mistake of asking him if his mother had done that, but mercifully recalled that no such cosy events could have figured in his childhood. He had only been a year old when his mother had taken off with her lover and never come back even for a visit. Unable to avoid answering her nosy questions, he had once told her that in a single derisive sentence that had pierced her tender heart.

When he was asleep, she went downstairs. She ate a beautiful meal in a superb dining room filled with enormous furniture. Her heart was too full to allow her thoughts to settle on anything other than Roel. It seemed obvious that before very long she would be going home again and instead of being happy at that possibility she felt unbearably sad because it meant that she was going to lose Roel again. He had already remembered something from those missing five years in his memory bank and it had happened even sooner than she had expected.

She had suspected that Dr Lerther was being rather too optimistic when he had repeatedly stated that Roel's amnesia would be of a very temporary nature. Now she could see that the consultant had been right on target with his forecast. Soon Roel would recall everything about the five years he had forgotten. He wouldn't need her any more. Had he ever really needed her? Or had that just been her own wishful thinking?

She curled up in a chair by the bed to watch over Roel while he slept. From now on, she told herself that she would ensure that their relationship remained strictly platonic. When he had remembered the truth about their supposed marriage how would he look at her? Would he think it strange that she had slept with him? Would he even care? He was a guy, a little inner voice protested soothingly. He was not going to waste loads of time agonising about *why* she might have done certain things. No, he would only want to get back into his real life. He would probably be very relieved to learn that, in strictly conventional terms, he did not really need to think of himself as a married man. In fact when he had regained his full memory he would most likely laugh at how events had developed.

When Hilary wakened she was lying in bed. Daylight was striking through a slender gap in the curtains and gleaming over Roel's proud dark head as he looked down at her. At some stage of the night he had stripped. His bare bronzed chest was just inches away from her and she was incredibly conscious of the hair-roughened masculine thigh lying against her own.

'What time is it?' she mumbled, taken aback by the fact that they were in the same bed again.

Brilliant dark golden eyes rested on her. 'Five after seven. I slept the clock round. I feel *amazing*…'

'I don't remember coming to bed—'

'You didn't. You were sleeping in the chair. You shouldn't worry so much about me, *cara*,' Roel reproved. 'I'm brilliant at looking after myself.'

The dark, husky timbre of his accented drawl shimmied down her taut spinal cord. Without responding to any conscious prompting, she found herself shifting even closer to him. It was like being possessed, she thought in panic at her own behaviour. There was to be no more intimacy, she reminded herself wretchedly, and in a sudden movement she made herself sit up.

'Without hesitation, Roel tipped her right back again, lean, strong face intent, smouldering dark golden eyes full of unashamed sexual hunger. 'You're not going anywhere, Signora Sabatino.'

If anything his use of that form of address made Hilary's conscience hurt even more. 'But—'

'You're very restless this morning.' Laughing, Roel slid a thigh between hers to anchor her in place beneath him. 'But you're not allowed out of bed until I say so.'

As she gazed up into his darkly handsome features her heart jumped and she felt weak with lust and longing. In the interim he brought his intoxicatingly sensual mouth down on hers. His hungry urgency sent her temperature rocketing.

Golden eyes bright with male appreciation, Roel bared her creamy rose-tipped breasts. Something pulled tight low in her pelvis and made her squirm up her hips. He cupped her swollen flesh, let knowing fingers play over her distended nipples and excited a low cry from her throat.

'You want me, *bella mia*,' Roel stated with satisfaction.

'Yes…' Hilary could not believe how fast it had become impossible to think, never mind fight what she was feeling. She craved his mouth and the erotic mastery of his touch. Her body was burning with impatience, eager and hot. That craving made it all the easier for her to suppress the little voice at the back of her mind that warned that she was doing wrong.

Eager for the hard demand of his mouth on her own, she rejoiced in his passion. She luxuriated in the right to shape his proud dark head, sink her fingers into the springy depths of his black hair and stroke her palms over the satin-smooth skin covering his muscular shoulders. She licked his skin there and thought he tasted sublime. Tingles of eager response shock-waved through her slender length and drove her to a fever pitch.

'You make me so hungry for you,' Roel growled and he flipped her over and into a position she didn't expect before he plunged into her with one driving thrust.

The wave of wicked pleasure took her in a stormy tide that made her whimper in shock at the delight of such sensation. The damp, sensitive place at the heart of her had become a fiery furnace. Ecstasy had her in its hold and there was no room for pride or shame in her passionate response. When the rush of sweet pleasure became unbearable, she surged into a shattering release with an abandoned cry, her excitement only heightened by the shudders of climax racking him in concert.

Still engulfed in the after shocks of rapture and with her eyes misted with happy tears, Hilary tumbled back against the pillows and held Roel's big powerful body close. He kissed her long and slow and deep and she struggled to catch her breath again.

She looked up at him, marvelling at his hard male beauty. A giant wave of love and appreciation was engulfing her. His slumberous dark golden eyes withstood her tender inspection and her fair skin warmed with self-conscious colour, but still she could not stop revelling in the very right to stare at him. High cheekbones slashed his bold dark features into proud planes and hollows. He was stunningly handsome even with dark stubble roughening his hard jaw line.

'You take my breath away…' she whispered shakily, laying her fingers against his wide, sensual mouth.

He caught her hand in his and then gazed down at her bare fingers with palpable surprise. 'Where's your wedding ring?'

Hilary froze in consternation. That a husband might reasonably expect his wife to be wearing a ring should have occurred to her, but it had not. 'I…er…I didn't want to wear one—'

Resting back against the pillows, Roel surveyed her with brooding intensity. 'Why not?'

Beneath that grim scrutiny, Hilary went scarlet and stammered, 'I—I just thought rings were a bit old-fashioned and didn't see why I should bother.'

'I don't like it,' Roel decreed without hesitation. 'I married you and I expect you to wear a wedding ring.'

Feeling horrible that she was allowing herself to tell more lies to protect her own masquerade, Hilary could no longer meet his gaze. 'I'll think that over.'

'No. You won't think anything over. I'll buy a wedding ring. You'll wear it. *End* of discussion,' Roel delivered with derisive force and sprang out of bed to pull on a pair of black silk boxer shorts.

Halfway across the room his long forceful stride came to a halt and he swung back to her. His lean dark face was impassive, his brilliant eyes decidedly challenging. 'You know, you never did tell me why my wife was still a virgin…?'

'And I'm not going to when you speak to me in that tone,' Hilary fielded, tautly defensive, sitting bolt upright in the vast bed, clutching the sheet round her as though it were her only sanctuary in the storm.

'You'll have to do better than that, *cara mia*,' Roel drawled.

Her eyes flashed and she stormed back at him in Italian. 'No, I don't! When you get your memory back you'll realise that there's no big mystery on the score of my lack of experience—'

'Is that a fact?'

'*And* you're not going to think it's remotely important either!' Hilary completed.

'Tell me just one thing,' Roel fired at her. 'Why did I marry you?'

Hilary stilled and finally muttered indistinctly, 'You married me for all the usual reasons...'

'Are you saying that I fell in love with you?' Roel demanded.

'I'm not saying anything...' Colliding unwarily with his shimmering dark golden eyes, she decided that she might as well tell him what he expected to hear so that the issue could be laid to rest. 'OK...you fell in love with me.'

Roel paced back a step towards her, his tension palpable. 'So I bought into the whole fairy tale?'

'Why not?' Hilary asked, her voice rising a little with strain.

'No reason.' Roel bent down and scooped her off the mattress. 'But if I went for the whole fairy tale, it means you'll definitely be the kind of woman who wants to share the shower with me,' he teased.

'Is that blackmail?' she dared unevenly.

Over breakfast in a charming sunlit courtyard orna-mented with lush flowering climbers and pots over-flowing with greenery, Hilary asked Roel about the history of the castle. That he loved every time-worn

stone was obvious to her. She tried not to think about
the lies she had told him earlier. He had stopped asking awkward questions and he was no longer concerned about their relationship. Since Dr Lerther had
advised her to give Roel nothing to worry about,
didn't that mean that she had done the right thing? A
couple of soothing little fibs was not going to cause
any lasting damage, she reasoned.

'I organised a surprise for you yesterday,' Roel revealed as he walked through the grand hall.

'What kind of a surprise?'

'I thought it was time to take care of the clothing
problem,' he told her softly and cast open the door
on a huge and crowded reception room.

Roel had issued invitations to several designer sa-
lons to visit the *castello* with a selection of garments.
Hilary was whisked into the room next door to have
her vital measurements taken and her attention fully
claimed. She was in a panic. How could she allow
Roel to go the expense of buying her an entire wardrobe? But how could she persuade him that she didn't
need anything new when he himself had seen how
seriously short of clothing she seemed to be?

Only minutes later she was paraded back into
Roel's presence. She was wearing a skirt suit that was
at the cutting edge of the latest fashion trends.

Roel studied her. The aqua shade flattered her fair
skin and bright silvery blonde hair while the short
fitted jacket and flirty skirt emphasised her stunning
hourglass figure and shapely legs. His keen gaze
glinted with masculine approval. 'Delectable,' he
murmured huskily for her ears alone.

And for the first time in her life Hilary felt worthy
of special attention. Her own imperfections seemed to

vanish beneath the balm of Roel's unashamed appreciation. She was blushing like mad and feeling hugely self-conscious but at the same time she held her head high and she felt proud. When Roel was admiring her, she could no longer lament her imperfect features, lack of height and too generous curves.

From that point on, Hilary was enjoying herself and existing in a realm in which Roel was her only focus. She tried on outfit after outfit. The expensive fabrics felt wonderfully luxurious against her skin. The tall gilded mirrors on the walls reflected her in a myriad unrecognisable guises. She saw herself twirl in a magnificent evening gown, a stunning trouser suit and a series of incredibly flattering little dresses, every one of which Roel seemed to signal a special liking for. Shoes and bags were produced to match. It was like a glorious dream in which everyone conspired to encourage her to play her favourite game of dressing-up just as she had when she was a little girl.

In the space of hours she acquired more clothes than she had ever owned in her whole life. She knew that she would never wear most of them and told herself that Roel would be able to return them once she had gone home again. She did, however, succumb to selecting several bra-and-pants sets as well as nightwear for she had packed nowhere near enough for her Swiss sojourn. Breathless and still on the crest of an excited wave, she kept on a cream skirt and a sleeveless draped top.

'I'm never going to wear all this stuff,' she warned Roel.

'You're my wife. You should have everything you want.'

Something twisted in the region of her heart and

her eyes shone overbright because she was so painfully aware of the pretence she was maintaining.

'Hilary?' Roel queried.

'You're being too generous to me,' she said tightly.

'Don't you know how to be generous in return?' Dazzling golden eyes flicked hers with sensual provocation and a scorching smile of devilment slanted his beautiful mouth.

Her heart hammered like a road drill and her mouth ran dry. He was so gorgeous he made her tremble. His power over her was terrifyingly strong but for a young woman who all her life had followed only her own counsel there was something deeply, disturbingly thrilling about his innately forceful temperament.

'And if you don't know…I can certainly give you hints, *bella mia*,' Roel purred with sensual huskiness.

She pressed her slender thighs together on the tingling responsive heat forming an ache of emptiness at the heart of her. Shocked at the strength of her own reactions, she lowered her eyes, fighting her own weakness as hard as she could.

But Roel drew her up against him. As she felt the taut power of his male arousal her face burned and yet she wanted to melt into him with every fibre of her being. Blazing golden eyes held hers. 'You look incredible, but what I want more than anything else in this world is for you to take those new clothes off again,' he confided raggedly.

Hilary moved back from him. She did something she'd thought she would never do. With unsteady hands she closed her fingers to the hem of her top and peeled it off. Then she unzipped her skirt, let it fall and stepped out of it.

'I suspect I married you because you keep on surprising me,' Roel commented rawly as he hauled her back to him with impatient hands and captured her mouth with devastating passion.

'It's out of this world.' Hilary's voice wavered. 'I just don't know what to say…I wasn't expecting this.'

She stroked a wondering finger over the delicate platinum band on her ring finger and gazed at Roel with dreamy gratitude. A wedding ring. She was touched to the heart that he should have wanted to see her wearing the symbol that signified marital commitment.

His brilliant dark golden eyes were level. 'I will not fail at anything, *cara*,' he admitted. 'I intend our marriage to be a success.'

A stab of discomfiture pierced the veil of fantasy behind which Hilary had buried all her misgivings about the role she was playing. For four whole days she had refused to think further than one minute into the future. She had revelled in every moment she had spent with Roel and if it was possible she had fallen even more deeply in love with him. He was bitterly frustrated by the reality that he had yet to recover his memory. The return of that one tiny recollection had only increased his impatience. But he had demonstrated extraordinary strength of character in the way he dealt with his amnesia and made her more than ever aware of his rock-solid assurance and self-discipline.

Now, made uneasy by his grave sincerity on the topic of their supposed marriage and wounded too by the wretched awareness of what she could not have, Hilary dragged her attention from his lean, extravagantly handsome features and made herself study her

Play The Lucky Hearts Game

and get...

FREE BOOKS & a FREE GIFT...

YOURS to KEEP!

Yes! I have scratched off the silver card. Please send me my **FREE BOOKS** and **FREE MYSTERY GIFT**. I understand that I am under no obligation to purchase any books as explained on the back of this card. I am over 18 years of age.

Scratch Here! then look below to see what you can claim...

P4CI

Mrs/Miss/Ms/Mr _____ Initials _____

BLOCK CAPITALS PLEASE

Surname _____

Address _____

_____

Postcode _____

Twenty-one gets you
4 FREE BOOKS and a
MYSTERY GIFT!

Twenty gets you
1 FREE BOOK and a
MYSTERY GIFT!

Nineteen gets you
1 FREE BOOK!

TRY AGAIN!

The Reader Service™ — Here's how it works:

NO STAMP NEEDED!

THE READER SERVICE™
FREE BOOK OFFER
FREEPOST CN81
CROYDON
CR9 3WZ

NO STAMP
NECESSARY
IF POSTED IN
THE U.K. OR N.I.

surroundings instead. After all, it was a gorgeous day
and the landscape was spectacularly beautiful. They
were sitting on the stone terrace of an exclusive restaurant set high above the lake at Lucerne. The sky
was a dense bright blue and the picturesque medieval
city was spread out below them.

'Hilary…?'

Roel reclaimed her attention with a frown just as a
broadly built man with earnest features and blonde
hair came to a halt several feet away and said, *'Roel?'*
in a tone of pleased surprise.

His rare smile forming, Roel immediately vaulted
upright to greet him. Hilary was aghast to recognise
the man as Paul Correro, who had acted as a witness
at their wedding. Sheer panic filled her and she was
paralysed to the spot by the lawyer's intent scrutiny.
This was someone who knew that she was a fake
wife, who had been paid to perform a service. He had
to be astonished to see her in Switzerland in Roel's
actual company!

CHAPTER SIX

HEART thumping out her state of alarm like a manic road drill, Hilary decided that she had no choice but to attempt to brazen the situation out.

'Anya and I are staying with friends,' Paul Correro was telling Roel, who was kissing the cheek of the pretty pregnant redhead standing by his lawyer's side.

Arrogant dark head turning, Roel cast Hilary a glance that queried her lack of participation. Perspiration beading her upper lip and a fixed smile on her tense mouth, Hilary got up from the table and moved forward on legs that felt as clumsy as solid wood.

'Hilary…' Paul Correro dealt her a smooth smile that somehow contrived to send a shiver of foreboding down her rigid spine. 'London's loss is our gain!'

At that gibe, Hilary almost flinched and she stood like a criminal waiting for the executioner's axe to fall. But Roel mercifully removed his lawyer's attention from her by engaging him in a low-pitched dialogue. As the two men lounged back against the stone balustrade several feet away, Paul's companion approached her.

'I'm Paul's wife, Anya,' she announced, her gaze coldly assessing.

'Yes.' Nervous as a cat on hot bricks and quite unable to think of anything to say in the face of that hostile appraisal, Hilary stole a strained glance over at Roel and Paul and wondered frantically what they

were talking about. An urgent desire for escape over-
came her and, with a muttered excuse, Hilary headed
for the cloakroom.

How dared Paul and Anya Correro look at her as
though she were some sort of criminal? She was hot
and bothered and her tummy was churning. She ran
cooling water over her hands while she fought to get
a grip on her seething emotions. Everything she had
done she had done for Roel's sake and, for a guy of
his temperament still frustrated by a five-year gap in
his memory, Roel was managing very well! But was
Paul Correro telling Roel right now that Hilary and
their apparent marriage were twin giant fakes?

Hilary emerged from the cloakroom only to find
Paul Correro waiting to corner her. Already pale, she
turned the colour of bleached bone.

'What's your game?' the blonde man demanded.
'Roel has just explained *why* he has barely been seen
since the accident.'

'I'm glad he's taken someone else into his confidence,' Hilary mumbled, wondering if Roel had already been told that she was not quite the wife she
had allowed him to believe she was. Her heart sank
like a stone.

'Don't treat me like an idiot,' Paul Correro condemned in a harsh undertone. 'The head of Roel's
security team called me yesterday to ask for my advice. Imagine how astonished I was to learn that *you*
had shown up at the clinic claiming to be Signora
Sabatino! This meeting is no coincidence. I interrupted my vacation to come here. How could you
think that you could pull a scam like this off?'

Beneath the lash of his scorn, Hilary was trembling.
A security team worked for Roel? They had been so

discreet she had had no idea of their existence. 'There hasn't been any scam. Have you told Roel the truth about our marriage?'

'In a restaurant?' the blonde man derided. 'I intend to call at the *Castello* this afternoon—'

Her eyes raw with appeal, Hilary closed a desperate hand over his sleeve. 'Let *me* tell Roel. Give me until tomorrow to sort all this out—'

'No. I'll give you until this evening. That's long enough, and if you don't keep your word I'll take care of it for you,' Paul Correro warned her, his distrust unconcealed.

It took enormous courage for Hilary to meet his accusing scrutiny. 'I'm not what you think I am. I love him. I've always loved him—'

The lawyer winced. 'Whatever,' he cut in dismissively. 'He'll never forgive this level of betrayal.'

In a daze, Hilary walked back to Roel's side. Anya was begging him to give a speech at some charity event. Paul joined his wife. Mentioning that they were running late for an appointment, Roel cut the dialogue short and swept Hilary back out to the limousine.

'Paul was in a weird mood.' A frown had hardened Roel's lean, strong face. 'Why was he so uncomfortable with you?'

'Oh, you know Paul,' she muttered weakly.

'I do. I know him well and he has never learned the art of deception. I sensed a certain disrespect in his attitude towards you,' Roel admitted. 'I found that offensive.'

Guilt pierced Hilary deep. She said nothing, saw that in the circumstances there was nothing she could say. Roel was an acute observer and he had noticed his lawyer's hostility. However, Roel would soon know and understand why Paul Correro had been unable to conceal his scorn. A heady combination of fear and despair overwhelmed Hilary. How could she face telling Roel that their marriage was not a real marriage? How could she possibly face doing that?

Only when the limo came to a halt outside an exclusive beauty salon did Hilary recall that the day before she had booked an appointment there. An appointment to get the pink tips removed from her hair because she had decided that her bi-coloured locks looked a little juvenile. Why not be honest with yourself? a little inner voice asked. She was ditching the pink tips in an effort to achieve a more elegant appearance for Roel. But what was the point now? What was the point when the bottom had just fallen out of her fantasy world?

'Hilary?' Roel prompted.

'Could we just drive round for a minute or two?' she gabbled without daring to look at him, for she was so confused she could hardly think straight. But she was aware of how reluctant she was to get out of the car and leave him.

The truth *hurt*. Who had first said that? She had no idea. She only knew that for the past week she had been foolish enough to try and live her dream. She had buried her every scruple and surrendered to the fairy tale of pretending to be Roel's wife. And she had been incredibly happy, happier than she had ever known she could be because the guy she loved had treated her as though she was the woman he had married. But the point was that she was not what he believed her to be and all the wishing in the world could not change that fact.

Paul Correro had destroyed her pathetic pretences.

He had also made her painfully aware that her actions could be judged in a harsh and self-serving light. But she had never intended to hurt or worry anyone. Even less would she have wished to cause the smallest harm to the guy she adored! However, just remembering how Paul Correro had looked at her brought Hilary out in a cold sweat. The cosy fantasy that had featured only Roel and her had been invaded and she had been plunged into terrible confusion.

'Do you want to skip this appointment?' Roel questioned with an edge of impatience.

He was so decisive. He could answer the average question before she had finished asking it. How would he feel about her when he realised that she had encouraged him to live a lie with her? Would he, as Paul Correro had implied, despise her for her behaviour? She was unbearably hurt by that idea but minute by minute an awareness that her masquerade had gone too far was bearing down on her. Perhaps her masquerade had gone too far the very instant she had lain in Roel's bed and allowed their relationship to become intimate.

'What—?'

'It's OK…I've made my mind up and I'm going to get my hair done!' Hilary proclaimed with a forced laugh as she turned to look at him.

Brilliant dark golden eyes telegraphed a mixture of impatience and wonderment over the strange way that her brain seemed to work when compared with his. Getting out of the car wasn't made any easier by the fact that he looked absolutely devastatingly gorgeous. In a sudden movement she skimmed across the seat and kissed him with bitter-sweet fervour.

'It's been such a wonderful few days…' she mumbled unsteadily, snatching up her bag and hurtling out of the limo before she could embarrass herself and him any further.

In the hairdressing salon she felt as though a glass wall separated her from the buzz of familiar activity. Dully she recognised that she was in shock. She also finally understood what her mind was so reluctant to confront and accept: it was time for her to bow back out of Roel's life again. She needed to leave quickly as well. What would be the point of returning to the *castello* to tell Roel what she had done? That would only plunge them both into an unpleasant confrontation and how was that likely to profit either of them?

She decided that it would be wiser to fly straight back home to London instead. Fortunately, she had kept her passport in her bag and once her hair was done she could head for the airport at Lugano. She had only brought a few clothes with her to Switzerland and what she was leaving behind would not be missed. She would leave a letter of explanation for Roel in the limousine. Wouldn't that be the most sensible choice? When he appreciated the truth of what she had done, he would be astonished and furious and probably consider himself very well rid of her. Any good opinion he had had of her would be utterly destroyed.

Her tight throat convulsed on the tears she was struggling to hold back. How on earth had things gone so very wrong? She had set out only to help Roel and had somehow got sucked in so deep that she had closed her eyes and ears to the promptings of her own conscience. She had allowed herself to get carried away with her own fantasy. Only now when she was forced to wonder how Roel would judge her behaviour did she appreciate that she had crossed the boundary line of what was honest and acceptable. That acknowledgement hit her very hard for Hilary never hid from her own mistakes. But on her terms the toughest punishment of all had to be the hard reality that she would never, ever see Roel again…

'Haven't you taken your break yet?' Sally Witherspoon asked Hilary.

Hilary set a pile of freshly laundered faded towels on the shelf behind the washbasins. 'I'm not hungry—'

'Well, you ought to be.' Her senior stylist's homely face was concerned. 'You can't work the hours you're working on an empty stomach. You look so tired.'

'Stop worrying about me. I'm fine.' Her silvery blonde head bent, Hilary got on with topping up the shampoo bottles as if her life depended on it. And in a sense her life did depend on activity because, the busier she kept herself, the less opportunity she had to brood. She knew that she had shadows under her eyes and that she was looking less than her best. She wasn't sleeping well and her appetite had vanished. She was horribly unhappy but she despised self-pity and was doing her utmost to behave normally and regain her spirits.

What was done was done. It was two weeks since she had flown back from Switzerland. For seven days Roel had been the centre of her world and now he wasn't there any more and he never would be again and she had to learn to live with that. But what she also needed to accept was that what she had shared with Roel had been unreal and false and that was the hardest lesson of all for her to bear.

'Your eleven o'clock appointment's here...' Sally hissed. 'He's a right good-looking bloke too...aren't you the lucky one?'

Hilary lifted her head. Roel was poised in the centre of the room. Her hand jerked the giant bottle of shampoo she was holding and the liquid began to pour down the sink instead of into the dispenser.

She was so shattered by the sight of him standing there that she gasped out loud. Her grey eyes locked to him with helplessly hungry intensity and she felt dizzy. Sheathed in a dark blue designer suit that outlined every lean, powerful line of his magnificent stature, his proud dark head at an angle, Roel was subjecting his surroundings to a keen scrutiny. He swung back, entrapping her mesmerised gaze. His dark-as-night eyes flared brilliant gold and glittered over her and he strolled fluid as a big cat towards her.

'Are you my eleven o'clock appointment?' she whispered.

Roel nodded in confirmation and subjected her rigid figure to a raking appraisal that drummed hot pink up into her cheeks. Clad in a white tee shirt and black cropped combat pants that hung low on her hips teamed with three-inch-high stiletto boots, Hilary discovered that she was suddenly alarmingly conscious of her every flaw. That sardonic inspection made her feverishly aware of her own body and of his deeply intimate acquaintance with it. Yet he had never looked at her before in quite that way. She realised that there was something different about him but did not know what it was. All she grasped was that she felt shamed.

'We need to go somewhere we can talk,' Roel murmured smooth and soft and for no reason at all that she could imagine her blood ran cold inside her veins.

'I'm…I'm…er…working,' she mumbled, a coward to the backbone at that instant.

'*Bene*…then I assume that you don't have a problem with your staff and your clientele hearing what I have to say to you.' Hard, handsome face merciless, Roel switched with fluid ease from his native Italian to English. 'I'll begin by admitting that I'm not impressed with the business I recall you set up with my money.'

Hilary almost cringed where she stood. But a split second later she was rocked by the ramifications of what he had just said. If Roel recalled their arrangement, he could no longer be suffering from amnesia. Since she had left Switzerland, Roel had evidently recovered his memory of those five lost years. Although his consultant had forecast exactly that conclusion, Hilary was severely shaken by the knowledge that Roel now remembered everything that had ever happened between them.

Her stomach churning with nervous tension, she turned aside to Sally and asked the other woman if she could cover her appointments until lunchtime.

'We can talk upstairs,' she told Roel tautly. 'When did you get your memory back?'

'After you disappeared. That probably helped. After all, you had me living a life that wasn't mine,' Roel pointed out sardonically.

Hilary paled at that unfeeling jibe and unlocked the door of her flat. 'I'm surprised you're here. I didn't think you'd want to see me again.'

The silence seethed. Roel sent the door flipping shut behind him. The hall was very narrow and dark and Hilary backed out of it into the kitchen/living room. Roel surveyed the worn furniture and general shabbiness and distaste flashed across his lean dark features.

'You're even poorer than I imagined. This place is a dump,' Roel pronounced in a grim undertone. 'When my foolish aunt, Bautista, contacted you when I was in hospital, the temptation to profit from my misfortune must have been overwhelming for you—'

'It was nothing of the sort!' Hilary was shattered by that accusation. 'How can you say such a thing? All I was worried about was you. For goodness' sake, I thought you were dying!'

Roel had lifted a letter lying on the table and he was reading it. He winced. 'You're in debt—'

Embarrassed to realise that he was looking at a communication from her bank urging her to settle the overdraft she had recently run up on her account, Hilary snatched it out of his hand again. 'Mind your own business!'

'Everything about you is my business. Knowing that gives me a good feeling,' Roel informed her with stinging softness.

Hilary had no idea what he was getting at and in any case was more keen to defend herself against the charge that she had gone to Switzerland in the hope of somehow enriching herself at his expense. 'Let me explain *why* I'm in debt. I spent a fortune on two very expensive last-minute flights to and from Switzerland and on paying extra wages to staff to cover for me while I was away. My budget doesn't run to extravagances like that.'

Unimpressed, Roel elevated a scathing ebony brow.

'Is poverty your only excuse for jumping at the opportunity to leap straight into my bed?'

Her hands balled into fists. 'You *put* me in that bed—'

'Oh, you really fought me off, didn't you?' Roel derided with a honeyed scorn that cut her like a knife blade. 'You're a conniving little con artist and you knew exactly what you were doing. Only by consummating our marriage could you ensure that you could claim a substantial divorce settlement from me.'

Hilary was bone-white. She felt horribly humiliated by his suspicions. 'I won't be claiming anything from you now or at any other time. I don't understand why you're thinking like this about me. Was it such a crime for me to want to see you when I heard you'd been injured? I told you I was sorry in my letter—'

Roel vented a sardonic laugh that made her flinch. 'All four lines of it? Even then you couldn't tell me the truth or admit the extent of your deception. You staged a vanishing act and you left me no explanation—'

'When it got down to it, I just didn't know what to say,' Hilary muttered tightly.

'You didn't want to warn me that I had been sharing my bed with a lying, cheating little whore?'

'Don't call me that!' Hilary launched back at him on a wave of angry hurt.

'You were a class act, *bella mia*.' Unforgiving golden eyes clashed with her anguished scrutiny and remained resolute. 'You knew the way to my heart…for an entire week you screwed my brains out every time I asked an awkward question!'

In a wild tempest of mortified pain at that wounding crack, Hilary snatched up the mug sitting on the table and threw it at him. 'That's not how it was; that *isn't* how I behaved!'

Offensively still, as though it was beneath his dignity to duck, Roel underlined his point by raising a speaking brow as the item hit the wall several feet to the left of him. 'When you're cornered you're very childish but that doesn't cut any ice with me. Neither do tears—'

'I'm not going to cry over you!' Hilary yelled at him full volume. 'You'd have to torture me to get tears!'

'Tears irritate me as do emotional scenes and flying pottery. But you should get it all out of your system now,' Roel advised grimly. 'If you make an ass of yourself in public again, I will be very angry with you.'

Growing stress was making Hilary's brow pound with a painful pulse-beat of tension. 'Make an ass of myself? *Again?* What are you talking about?'

Roel removed something from the inside pocket of his well-cut jacket and tossed it down on the table for her perusal. It was a magazine clipping and she was aghast to recognise the woman in the photo, who was clearly dashing tears from her unhappy face, as being herself. It had been taken that last day in Switzerland when she was walking into the airport at Lugano and she had not even noticed the photographer. Beneath ran several lines of French.

'What does it say?' Hilary finally prompted.

'"All that money and still miserable,"' Roel translated grittily.

Hilary folded her arms. 'Well, I'm sorry if I embarrassed you but it does prove that I was upset about the situation we'd got into—'

Roel dealt her a chilling glance. '*We?* Who created that situation? Who claimed to be my wife? Who lied her way into my home and my trust?'

Hilary unfolded her arms again with a jerk. Her eyes were bright with appeal and discomfiture. 'Look, try to understand that I just got in too deep. When I arrived in Switzerland I genuinely did think you were seriously hurt and I did really want to see you. I also believed you'd been asking for me—'

'Why the hell would I have been asking for a woman I had not seen in almost four years? A woman who meant nothing to me?' Roel demanded. 'And how could I have been asking for anyone while I was unconscious?'

Absorbing that salient fact for herself, Hilary's troubled face tightened with chagrin. Yes, it did indeed sound highly unlikely that he would have been asking for her. Had her sister, Emma, told her a little white lie? Had Emma made up that touching assurance in a naive attempt to encourage her elder sister to rush over to Geneva to be with her husband?

But before Hilary could fully consider that possibility Roel's own words sounded afresh inside her head in the cruellest of echoes. *A woman who meant nothing to me?* That was what he had said. That was how he thought of her. As nothing and nobody. Well, what had she expected? Tender affection? For the brief space of a week her pretences had led him to believe that he must have some feelings for her and he had behaved accordingly. But that comforting time was now at an end.

Determined not to betray how terribly hurt she was, Hilary struggled to get back to the point she had been intending to make before his casually cruel honesty had hit her like a punch in the stomach. 'Dr Lerther warned me not to tell you anything that might disturb you—'

'So you let me think I was married? Didn't that strike you as *very* disturbing news to give a man who revelled in being single?' Roel slammed back at her.

'I expect you really appreciate your freedom now that you know you never lost it—'

'I did not lose my freedom. You stole it from me.' His stunning golden eyes were full of contempt. 'You claimed to be my wife and now rumours abound that I am a married man. As, strictly speaking, I *am* a married man, I cannot deny those rumours and the paparazzi have already managed to print a photograph of you.'

Guilty tears lashed the back of Hilary's eyes. 'I suppose that has to be embarrassing for you—'

'I don't embarrass easily,' Roel cut in drily.

'I don't think you understand just how sorry I am,' Hilary mumbled wretchedly.

'Sorry is not enough to satisfy me. You really wanted to be my wife.'

Hilary's pallor became laced by feverish, embarrassed colour.

Roel sent her a sizzling look of scorn. 'You wanted to be my wife so badly that you lied and you cheated your way into the position.'

Shame and anger at the humiliation he was inflicting roared through Hilary. 'I know it looks bad but—'

'I won't listen to your excuses. It looks bad because it *was* bad,' Roel incised. 'You took my beautifully organised life and trashed it. I dumped my mistress for you—'

'You did…what?' Eyes widening, Hilary glanced up at him.

'The gorgeous brunette…she was my mistress and I ditched her because you made me believe that I was a married man.'

Hilary just closed her eyes. *The gorgeous brunette.* How could she ever have allowed herself to believe that a male like Roel Sabatino had no other woman in his life and his bed? She hadn't wanted to accept that there might be a woman because accepting that would have made her own position untenable. Wasn't that why she had chosen to assume that Roel was free of any entanglement? How could she have been so naive when it came to her own motives and so selfish? She really had messed up his life. Guilt and shame tore at her and made her throat thicken.

'So there is a current vacancy in my bed and you are about to fill it again.'

'I beg your pardon…?' A frown of incomprehension had formed on Hilary's strained face.

'You're coming back to Switzerland with me—'

Hilary was bemused. 'Why would I do that?'

'I'm not giving you a choice. Did you give me one when you told me that I was living in a fairy-tale marriage?' Roel shot at her with cold condemnation.

Hilary paled as if she had been struck and evaded his harsh gaze. 'I can't think of one good reason why you'd want me to come back to Switzerland—'

'I want to use you as you used me and then throw you away again when I get bored. Does that clarify the issue?' Lean, strong face hard, Roel met her shocked stare levelly.

Hilary released a dazed little laugh. 'You don't mean that…'

'I've arranged for us to lunch with your sister, so you should start packing.'

Hilary froze. 'How could we be meeting Emma for lunch? She's at a school miles out of London—'

'As we speak she's being driven down for the occasion.'

'But how…I mean why would you make such an arrangement?'

'I had excellent reasons. Did you think you were the only one of us who could pull a dirty trick? I'm a master at manipulation, *bella mia*.' Roel dealt her a look of pity. 'Emma thinks we're enjoying a reconciliation and she is ecstatic at the news, so you'll have to come up with loads of smiles and lots of that bouncy chatter at which you excel to keep her happy—'

Hilary's skin had turned clammy with shock. 'How the heck could you have even got in touch with my sister?'

'She phoned me at the town house this week and very touchingly apologised for her hostile attitude when we first got married.'

'Oh, no…' Hilary groaned in guilty dismay because she realised that it was her own fault that Emma had contacted Roel. Since her return from Switzerland, Hilary had only spoken to her sister on the phone and she had ducked all the younger woman's questions about the state of her relationship with Roel. Unable to tell the truth, she had not been able to bring herself to tell lies. 'I never did get round to admitting to her *why* we got married because I was scared…well scared—'

'That she might be less respectful of a sister who marries a man for money?' Roel slotted in with cruel accuracy. 'You'll be relieved to know that I left all her illusions intact. She told me how upset she was that we appeared to be living apart again and asked if that was her fault.'

'And what did you say…that we were having a reconciliation?' Hilary recalled with a visible effort to overcome her disbelief. 'Was that what you said a moment ago?'

'We *are* having a reconciliation…on my terms, and if they turn out to be on the punitive side of vengeful you only have yourself to thank for that.'

'You think I'm a lying, cheating, horrible person…I'd have to be out of my mind to go anywhere with you!' Hilary flung at him.

'*Non c'e problema*…don't worry about it,' Roel urged. 'I'll take your sister out to lunch on her own and tell her the entire unlovely story of our relationship from start to finish—'

'That would be a rotten, nasty thing to do!' Hilary broke in, her horror unconcealed.

'Unlike you, I would only be telling the truth as it happened. I'm relieved that you appreciate just how inexcusable your conduct has been,' Roel spelt out grimly as he left the room.

Hilary raced out into the hall in his wake. 'If you want me to grovel, I will, but don't drag Emma into this—'

Roel gave her a sardonic glance. 'Grovelling is for peasants and you should know me well enough by now to know that when I want something, I take it. You're going to learn how to be a Sabatino wife and you'll save me the time and effort of picking out another mistress by taking on the role personally—'

'No way!' Hilary yelled at him.

'But you worked so hard to get yourself into that position. Not indispensable, you understand,' Roel asserted drily, striding back to the front door and pulling it open, 'but certainly worth a return visit.'

'You wouldn't dare tell Emma what I did,' Hilary told him.

'I *would*…'

A chill of apprehension enclosed her. 'But doing that wouldn't profit you in any way. Why would you be so cruel?'

'It's what you deserve.' Roel studied her with brooding dark intensity. 'You conned me into giving you a wedding ring and, before I kick you back out of my life again, I intend to level the score.'

'I didn't con you…I *didn't*—'

Roel did not appear to be listening. 'A limo will collect you in an hour and a half and deliver you to the hotel where we're lunching with Emma. I'll meet you there. I'm calling into my London office first.'

Hilary was panicking. 'If I leave my business again, I'll be risking bankruptcy and I can't do that because—'

Roel gave her a withering look. 'I'll settle your debts—'

Hilary bridled. 'It's a two-hundred-and-fifty-pound overdraft run up on air fares…all right, it's money I owe, but stop talking like it's—'

'I'm a banker. An unauthorised overdraft is a debt—'

'You can't *do* this to me, Roel.' In her desperation, Hilary followed him out onto the landing. 'If I leave London, who's going to take my place while I'm away?'

'You hire a manager. I'll cover the expense—'

In furious frustration and lingering disbelief, Hilary watched Roel start down the stairs. 'If you use my relationship with my sister as a threat, I will never forgive you,' she warned him.

Lean, intelligent face cold and impassive in cast, Roel cast her a darkling glance. 'You think I'd care about that?'

Chilled, she slumped back against the wall and slowly breathed in deep in an effort to calm herself. He might even be glad of the excuse to punish her by revealing all to Emma. It was not a risk she could afford to run. She thought her sister might understand why she had signed up for such a marriage almost four years back when their lives had been so bleak, but she would be very hurt that Hilary had allowed her to believe that their marriage was a genuine one. To that injury would be added the facts of Hilary's more recent behaviour and how would Emma view that? Dear heaven, would Roel let Emma realise that Hilary had actually slept with him this time around? Hilary literally writhed with horror at the idea of having her own failings paraded for her kid sister's benefit. She was supposed to set standards for her younger sibling, not break them.

Roel had, with merciless precision, chosen the one threat capable of making Hilary dance to his tune…

CHAPTER SEVEN

'I'M JUST so happy for you!' Emma hugged Hilary with bubbling enthusiasm between the first and second courses of their meal. 'When I start university after the summer, you'll see even less of me and I was worried you'd get lonely. Does that sound selfish?'

'Of course it doesn't,' Hilary reassured her with as bright a smile as she could manage. Living away from home had made her sister independent and, although it hurt a little sometimes that Emma relied more on her own judgement, Hilary was very proud of her.

'Hilary needs to have some fun,' Emma informed Roel earnestly. 'She's given up so much for me. My scholarship only ever covered part of my school fees and Hilary's been paying the rest. That's why she's always so broke. When I realised how much my education was costing, I tried to persuade her to move me—'

'You were doing really well where you were and that was the most important thing,' Hilary slotted into that embarrassing flood of personal information being freely proffered to Roel. 'Emma wants to be an international lawyer. She's really good at languages.'

Roel spoke to her sister in French and Emma responded with impeccable cool. They both had that confident sharp edge that Hilary had always rather envied in others. After the meal, Roel took a call on his mobile and Hilary and her sister had a few minutes alone. Emma was returning to school to revise for her A-level exams. Once they were over, she was flying straight out to Spain to stay with a friend at her family's holiday villa. Having waved off her sister, Hilary climbed into the limo with Roel.

'I haven't finished sorting things out yet, so I'll have to go back to my flat.'

Roel sent her a hard glance. 'We don't have time.'

Hilary lifted her chin. 'You don't but I do. Fly me out economy tomorrow.'

'I'll reschedule our flight for later this evening—'

'That's not necessary,' Hilary said woodenly. 'I need more time to organise things. I'd prefer to travel tomorrow.'

Roel surveyed her mutinous profile. 'I'm not leaving London without you.'

'I don't want to go to Switzerland—'

'Liar,' Roel murmured huskily.

Hilary bristled. 'What's that supposed to mean?'

Roel ran a taunting forefinger along the generous curve of her lower lip. Her sensitive skin tingled and her breath caught in her throat.

'Show me how much you hate what I do to you, *bella mia*,' Roel suggested in a silken invitation.

Even though she was trying to fight the impulse, she found herself leaning forward. He drew her like a fire when she was freezing cold. Her nostrils flared on the achingly familiar scent of him: masculine overlaid with a trace of some expensive lotion, incredibly sexy. Her breasts stirred inside her bra cups, tender crests straining into stiff points.

'You're not trying hard enough,' Roel censured.

'Trying what?' Her mind was a total blank, her voice hoarse with the effort required to speak.

He raised a lean brown hand and stroked a provocative fingertip over the taut prominence of an engorged nipple outlined by the thin fabric of her top.

When he touched that sensitive peak a soft whimper of sound broke from her. Her heart was pounding like a drum. Her head felt too heavy for her neck and she let it tip back. Between her slender thighs the heat of wanting rose to a bitter-sweet peak of craving that burned.

Roel let the tip of his tongue flick the delicate hollow at the base of her collar-bone where a tiny pulse was going crazy and she moaned and pushed forward. She wanted him to kiss her so badly that she could taste it. He lifted his dark head and she looked up at him. Framed by impenetrable black lashes, the hard sexual glitter of his brilliant gaze was the equivalent of an electrical charge.

'Do it…' she was finally reduced to pleading.

'No. I'm not into sex in the back of limos.' Roel withdrew from her with a pronounced air of derision.

Her cheeks burned like beetroot on the boil. Her hands balled into fierce fists. She wanted to hit him. She wanted to say very rude things to him. But just in time she restrained herself from a revealing outburst. She was mortified by her own vulnerability. How could she have been so weak? *Show me how much you hate what I do to you!* If she continued to offer herself up on the equivalent of a plate to Roel, he would soon guess that she was head over heels in love with him. And, in Hilary's opinion, nothing would be worse than that development and nothing would be more humiliating. Given a choice, she decided that she much preferred to be thought of as a cunning gold-digger.

The limo pulled up outside the hairdressing salon and Hilary fled. While Sally grabbed a much-needed break, Hilary worked. Just before closing time, the older woman agreed to manage the salon as long as there was enough cash in the kitty to hire another full-time stylist to work alongside her. Relieved that she would be leaving her business in reliable hands, Hilary locked up, went over the account books with Sally and then went up to her flat to finish her packing.

At seven o'clock the doorbell sounded. Although she had assumed it was Roel, it wasn't. Her visitor was Gareth, an engineer, whom she had dated a couple of times the previous year and who had become a friend.

'*Love* the hair!' Gareth laughed and ruffled the glossy black tips that provided such a contrast to her silvery fair hair. 'Very gothic.'

'You like it?' Hilary grinned for Roel had not even seemed to notice and in truth it hardly mattered as the black highlights would wash straight back out of her hair again the next time she was under the shower.

'Fancy going out tonight?'

Lean, dark features grim, Roel strode across the landing. 'Hilary has other plans.'

'Are you her social secretary…or something?' Gareth sniped.

'Her husband,' Roel drawled with cold finality.

As Gareth clattered red-faced downstairs Hilary knew he would never darken her doorstep again and she slung Roel a furious look of reproach for his interference. 'That was quite unnecessary—'

From the benefit of his commanding height, Roel

dealt her a strong glance of disagreement. 'You were flirting—'

'I wasn't flirting…and even if I was, what's it got to do with you?' With difficulty Hilary controlled her temper because Roel's chauffeur had appeared round the bend in the stairs. Her cases were removed from the hall and she locked up with a flourish.

'You were expecting that guy tonight. That was why you didn't want to leave until tomorrow,' Roel condemned in a harsh undertone.

Hilary tossed her head on her passage down the first flight of stairs. But he was making her feel as irresistible as Helen of Troy and she glowed. 'I'm a real hot chick. You'll have to watch me night and day in Switzerland. Are you sure I'm worth the effort?'

Without the smallest warning, Roel closed his hands to her slight shoulders and backed her up against the wall of the landing. It happened so fast and so disconcerted her that she gasped. Volcanic golden eyes obdurate as bronze raked over her startled face in stormy warning. 'Have you noticed something? I'm not laughing,' Roel derided with raw-edged softness. 'Be careful. If I catch you flirting with other men, I won't be amused.'

Her mouth had run dry and, taken aback though she was by his vehemence, a dark and dangerous excitement was licking through her slight figure. 'I was just joking—'

'That wasn't funny,' Roel delivered darkly.

Her lively sense of humour sparked. 'At least Gareth noticed I'd put black tips into my hair—'

'Only he was too much of an oil slick to tell you that you look like a hedgehog.' Releasing her, Roel took a fluid step back to let her go on down the stairs.

Hilary drew in a shattered breath. *'A…?'*

A hedgehog? She was mortified. Passing through the airport, she could not help stealing glances at her reflection in shop windows. At the same time she could not help noticing how short and dumpy she looked alongside his tall, lean physique. While they waited to board Roel's private jet, Hilary's mobile phone buzzed. When she heard her friend Pippa's voice, she moved away from Roel to keep the conversation private.

Pippa and her husband, Andreo D'Alessio, lived in Italy and, as luck would have it, Pippa was calling to tell Hilary that she would be over in London for the weekend and was looking forward to meeting up with her.

'As we speak, I'm waiting to board a flight to Switzerland,' Hilary admitted ruefully. 'You're also going to have every excuse to get annoyed with me. I've been keeping a secret from you. I'm married—'

'Married? I don't believe you!' Pippa exclaimed in shock.

'He's standing right by me listening in on my phone call so I don't find it quite so hard to disbelieve,' Hilary confided tartly, slinging Roel a challenging glance. 'But the story of our marriage is—'

Roel filched the phone from her in a move so fast it left her with a dropped jaw. 'A total fairy tale,' Roel dropped in faster than the speed of light as he took over the dialogue without skipping a beat. 'I'm Hilary's husband…and you are—?'

Outraged, Hilary hovered while Roel engaged in smooth chit-chat with her friend and then deftly concluded the dialogue by announcing that their flight had been called.

'How *dare* you?' Hilary bit out in a tremulous voice, so mad she was shaking with fury as Roel escorted her across the tarmac towards the jet.

'*Dannazione!* You left me with no choice.' Scornful golden eyes skimmed over her angry face. 'You were on the brink of blabbing everything—'

'I don't "blab",' Hilary forced out between gritted teeth.

'You could blab for England. You have the discretion of a public address system,' Roel contradicted icily.

On board the jet, Hilary stalked down the aisle of the luxurious cabin and picked a seat as far away from him as she could get. She was furious that he had interfered with her call and accused her of being a gossip. How dared he?

'Just who do you think you are?' she heard herself demand when they were airborne and the steward had left them alone again.

Darkly handsome face unapologetic, Roel held her accusing gaze with level cool. 'I am a very private individual. What happens between us should be equally private. Girlie chatterbox sessions are out.'

Hilary turned her head away and curled up in her comfortable seat. Tears were not her style but all of a sudden she felt as though she could weep a river dry. Perhaps that was because she was feeling so tired that it was an effort to keep her heavy eyes open. The steward tried to interest her in a meal and she shook her head, her tummy reacting with a queasy roll at the prospect of food. She wanted to fight with Roel but for once she had to acknowledge that she did not have the energy.

The following morning, Hilary slept late. When she woke up she was eager to confront Roel with all the arguments she had been too enervated to employ when lunching with her sister, Emma, had been on the agenda. Over breakfast Umberto informed her that Roel had long since departed for the Sabatino Bank.

Her recollection of how she had got to bed the night before was dim but embarrassing. Having dozed through the flight, she had stumbled like a zombie through the airport, drifted off again in the limo and had allowed Roel to cart her up to bed when they had finally arrived at the town house. Never before had she suffered from such overpowering fatigue and it was a relief to feel the restored spark of her usual energy.

She had thought that she was really really hungry but when the cooked breakfast that she had ordered arrived her appetite suffered a sudden mysterious disappearance. Pushing away the plate, she nibbled at a fresh roll and savoured a hot chocolate drink, which was sinfully rich and satisfying. Having decided that a visit to that holy of holies, the Sabatino Bank, required a special effort in the grooming department, she was relieved to discover all the designer clothes that Roel had bought for her stowed away in the dressing room. She donned a burgundy lace slip dress, which took on a much more conservative aspect when teamed with a short floral cotton coat.

The Sabatino Bank in Geneva was hugely intimidating in size and very contemporary in design. Her nervous tension began to increase. Explaining that she was Roel's wife created a decided stir of discreet interest at the reception desk. A young man in a smart suit escorted her up to the executive floor. He showed her through double doors into a very large office.

Roel was lounging back with tigerish grace against the edge of a sleek light wood desk. Garbed in a dark blue tailored suit, grey shirt and stylish silk tie, he looked nothing short of spectacular. 'Fill me in,' he invited softly. 'It's not anyone's birthday. To what do I owe this interruption? What is the special occasion?'

'I just wanted to speak to you—'

'Then you should get out of bed earlier,' Raul spelt out drily. 'This is the middle of my working day and I am not available for personal visits.'

'That's good…cos this is a business call,' Hilary informed him, hoping to really grab his attention with that declaration.

Role vaulted upright and extended an authoritative lean brown hand. 'Come here. I want to show you something.'

Disconcerted, Hilary moved forward. He closed a hand over hers and proceeded to urge her towards a door on the other side of his office. 'Where are you taking me?'

It was a washroom. Stepping behind her, Roel posed her in front of the vanity unit, so that she could see their reflections twinned in the mirror above the basin. Her grey eyes focused on his lean bronzed face. Pulses quickening and heart racing, she sucked in an audible breath.

'What do you see?' Roel asked as he tipped the light coat off her taut shoulders and slowly removed it.

Hilary was mesmerised. 'Us?'

As though to draw attention to them, Roel flicked

the narrow beaded straps of her dress, which bared her slender shoulders. Then his long fingers glided from her tiny waist up over her narrow ribcage to rest just below the burgeoning thrust of lush breasts enhanced by the flattering fit of the stretchy lace fabric. Hilary stopped breathing altogether. At that precise moment the reason why she had come to Roel's office was a complete blank to her. His big powerful body was touching hers and she was infinitely more aware of his bold masculine arousal.

'Is this how a woman dresses for a business appointment, *cara*?' Roel enquired silkily.

'I know the dress is a bit flirty but I love it, so I put the coat on top of it so that I would look more conservative,' Hilary told him breathlessly.

'That's not the point I was making. Just for the record, put a dress like that over a shape like yours and the result could not be described by any stretch of the imagination as...*conservative*.'

Hilary leant back into him and gave him a huge dreamy smile. 'You like it?'

'Isn't that what you wanted?'

'I didn't think about it but you're probably right.'

A superior gleam in his brilliant golden eyes, Roel set her back from him with gentle but firm hands. 'So this scene belongs in the bedroom, not inside my bank.'

Absorbing that speech, Hilary blinked on the sizzle of pure rage that lit up like a neon sign inside her. He actually thought that she had come to his precious bank to try and seduce him away from a working ethic set in ancient stone!

'I came here to have a serious discussion,' Hilary snapped and, stooping to pick up her coat, she stalked back into his office. 'And I intend to have that discussion. Sorry if you can't keep your mind on business just because a woman's wearing an attractive dress.'

Dark colour girding his proud high cheekbones, Roel sent her a slashing glance. 'Try me…'

'Almost four years ago, I signed a contract to become your wife. In return I accepted a certain sum of money. I returned two thirds of that sum when I discovered I didn't need it and—'

Roel had raised a silencing hand. 'Stop there. You *returned* part of that cash settlement? How?'

'I paid it back into the account you had set up and sent you a letter through your lawyer, that suspicious Paul guy—'

'Who had great foresight,' Roel sliced in with satiric bite. 'Thanks to your antics, I broke his nose last week—'

Eyes rounded, Hilary stared at him in consternation. 'You did what…you broke his nose? But why?'

'He had the misfortune to suggest that my wife might not be all that I believed her to be…*before* I recovered my memory.'

Hilary turned bright pink with mortification. 'Oh…I was talking about that money.'

Roel looked unimpressed. 'I'm not aware that you returned any part of that settlement.'

Hilary folded her arms with a jerk. 'Well, the point is that I did. I realised that I didn't need to buy a property when renting one would do just as well. I only kept what I needed to rent the flat and set up the salon in the empty shop beneath it. Fitting out the salon was expensive enough. You didn't think my business was much of a paying proposition but it pays my rent and covers the bills, so I've never had any complaints—'

'Would you tell me where this dialogue is heading?'

'Once Emma finishes school, I can sell the business as a going concern and repay everything you gave me. So if I put that promise on the table, we'll be quits and you can let me go home again.'

'Did you really put on your sexiest outfit to come and make that offer to me?'

Infuriated by a putdown of a response that made it clear that he did not even deem her offer worthy of consideration, Hilary breathed in very deep. Meanwhile, Roel lounged back against his desk, watching the rise and fall of her full breasts below the lace and then whipping up again to rest on her luscious pink mouth.

'As far as I'm concerned, this isn't about money. It never has been. Surely you've grasped that by now?' Roel murmured softly.

'I understand that you believe I owe you a debt. I understand that you have rather unforgiving principles—'

'You're doing really well on the understanding front,' Roel dropped in with deflating amusement.

'But I can't think of one good reason why you'd want to force me to be here—'

Roel sent her a sardonic smile. 'But I've got *more* than one good reason. The power kick. I am receiving very real satisfaction from making you do what I want you to do.'

'That's disgusting…you should be ashamed of yourself!' Hilary was outraged that he could admit that without hesitation.

His stunning eyes narrowed intently. 'But didn't *you* receive a similar satisfaction when you took advantage of my amnesia to lull me into a false sense of security?'

'I'm not like you…I didn't take advantage either!' Hilary flung at him, hurt by that unpleasant suggestion. 'I was only trying to keep you calm and happy.'

His handsome mouth quirked with amusement. '*Per meraviglia*…you certainly put a smile on my face in the bedroom. As for forcing you to be here, isn't it time you faced facts?'

'What facts?'

'That you didn't exactly have to be dragged kicking and screaming back to my lair? You want me too.'

'Not enough to allow you to think you can use me,' Hilary stated hotly.

Roel let his forefinger slowly glance down between her breasts to pause at her navel. 'What would be enough?'

Where he stroked, her body became stingingly alive and tender. It was as if her every skin cell lit up.

She set her teeth together and trembled. 'Sex isn't enough for me.'

'I could make it enough,' Roel informed her huskily.

'I value myself more.'

'Yet you didn't four years ago. If I'd snapped my fingers then you would have come running.'

She was devastated by that crack. For an instant she was torn from the present and plunged back into the past. She had been so desperately in love with him and without hope. She had been young and foolish and she would have done just about anything to get a chance with him. To be forced to accept that he had known exactly how she felt then and yet still walked away from her was unbearably painful.

'You bastard...' she framed jaggedly. 'You were attracted to me too but you wouldn't do anything about it—'

'I was too sensible—'

'Too much of a snob,' Hilary contradicted with wounded and angry blue eyes. 'I bet if I'd been some spoilt little debutante you would have given me a spin!'

'I'm not a snob. I have expectations in certain fields and I don't apologise for them—'

'You're the guy who was born with an entire silver service in his mouth. All your life you have had the best and you looked at me and you felt the same attraction I did...I *know* you did!' Hilary stressed in a mixture of furious and hurt accusation. 'Because you admitted that to me while you had amnesia—'

'I walked away because you couldn't have handled me. You were too young—'

'You walked away because you have a brain that functions like a deep freeze—'

'Is that your definition of common sense?' Roel drawled silkily.

'—and because I didn't fit the right image—'

'You still don't...yet here you are.' Dark drawl razor-edged, Roel curved controlling hands to the shapely curve of her hips and drew her to him.

'You think kissing me is somehow going to make me less furious with you?' Hilary threw at him tempestuously.

He did it anyway. He crushed her soft mouth under his and then lingered to demand a greater response.

He teased at the full curve of her lower lip and she shivered, abruptly leaning forward to brace her hands on his hard, muscular shoulders. He stopped teasing, hauled her close and plundered the tender interior of her mouth with driving explicit strokes that made the blood drum through her veins at an insane rate.

'I can't wait until seven tonight,' Roel growled thickly, pausing to nip at the lobe of her ear with his teeth before burying his carnal mouth in the hollow of her neck.

'Oh…' In reaction to that contact, an incredibly erotic sensation darted through her and she snatched in a startled breath. He wasn't supposed to be kissing her, she reminded herself. She was angry with him, she reminded herself. But she curled her nails like talons into the expensive fabric of his suit jacket and found his tempting masculine mouth again for herself.

Roel released the back zip on her dress and cool air washed her spine. She fought to catch her breath while the lace fabric shimmied down over her hips into a pool at her feet. 'No…you can't do that!' Hilary gasped in shock.

'Too late…' Roel framed thickly.

Hilary whipped up her hands in a genuine effort to cover herself. She was in a panic. 'We're in a bank…any minute now someone might come through that door!'

'It's locked…we're safe.' With single-minded purpose, Roel tugged her hands back down to her side. He tipped back his handsome dark head to better appreciate the sight of her luxuriant curves embellished by a frivolous bra and panties. 'But you're *not*…'

As Hilary began to stoop to reach for her dress Roel lifted her up into his arms with easy strength.

He brought her down on the desk and flipped loose the catch on her bra. 'Roel!'

'Irresistible…' Roel surveyed the pouting perfection of her pink-tipped breasts and groaned out loud.

Smouldering golden eyes met hers and the raw hunger she saw there shook her. His uninhibited desire lit a fire inside her. He might not love her but his passion was very real. Emboldened, she angled up on one elbow and tugged him down to her by his silk tie.

Lean, strong face hard with male need, he vented a roughened Italian imprecation. '*Inferno!* You're in my blood like a fever.'

He curved his hands to the ripe swell of her breasts, making her moan soft and low. He rubbed her tightly beaded nipples and she gasped in helpless response. Liquid heat started to gather at the apex of her thighs. He let his expert mouth wander at will across her sensitised flesh and all thought was suspended. Her hips gave a restive upward surge and he sank his hands beneath them to bring her even closer.

A phone began buzzing. He swore, reached behind her and the noise stopped. He laced long fingers into her hair, holding her to him while he drove her lips apart with the demanding force of his passion.

'I want you,' she muttered, snatching in a frantic shallow breath, her whole body thrumming with passionate need.

'Not as much as I want you, *bella mia*,' Roel ground out, ripping off her last garment with more haste than care. 'You've taught me that two weeks can feel like two lifetimes.'

He spread her thighs and discovered the hot, damp ache of her most secret flesh. As he explored her slick, wet heat a sobbing sound of frustration was wrenched from her and she arched in a frenzy of helpless impatience. Positioning her with strong hands, he plunged into her in one powerful movement. It was intolerably exciting. A surging wave of pleasure splintered through her. All control was gone. He was taking her to the outer limits of an exquisite peak of sensation. When it claimed her in a wild climax of shattering intensity, he smothered her cries with the cloaking heat of his mouth.

In the aftermath she was shell-shocked by her own abandonment.

Withdrawing from her, Roel stared down at her with stunned golden eyes. 'I can't believe we just did this…I can't believe you're lying naked across my desk.'

It needed only that one reminder for Hilary to recall both her surroundings and her unclothed state. She leapt off his desk like a scalded cat. She wanted to crawl under it and hide but not before she got herself decently covered again. Fighting hands that were all fingers and uncoordinated thumbs, she struggled back into her bra and pants. All around her the silence seethed.

'You're banned from my office,' Roel drawled coolly.

'Sorry…s-say that again,' she stammered weakly, engaged in hauling up her dress with frantic hands.

'I think you staged a deliberate power play. You came here dressed to kill with a purpose,' Roel condemned with outrageous cool.

Hilary almost flung herself at him sobbing with raging hysteria. He thought she had planned her own downfall? He thought she was proud of having been spread-eagled across his desk? Was he out of his mind? Face bright red with shame, she wriggled in an agitated effort to pull up her zip for herself.

'From the minute I came through that door, you had only one thought in your mind. Don't you dare blame me...thanks,' she muttered in absent aside as, noticing her acrobatic twists, he flipped her round and took care of her zip. 'Who locked the door? Who ignored me when I tried to remind you of where we were? Who told me two weeks without sex is like two lifetimes?'

'Hilary—'

'And the same second you get what you want, you start acting like I threw myself at you,' she ranted at him feverishly, because while she was still shouting and simultaneously heading in the direction of the door she could pretty much avoid looking at him. 'Who flattened me on that desk with lustful intentions? Believe me, wild horses wouldn't get me back inside this bank!'

Roel swept up her coat and extended it.

'You've got lipstick on your shirt,' she told him with considerable satisfaction.

Glittering golden eyes ensnared hers with bold determination. 'Can we do this again soon?'

Hilary stared at him in mortified disbelief. 'After you virtually accused me of setting this up?'

'I'd like to set you up for a repeat visit, *cara mia*.'

'Dream on!' Hilary flung at him.

'I'm a connoisseur,' Roel murmured smoothly. 'And sex that good is rare.'

Paling, Hilary veiled her eyes and dropped her head. He was so unemotional. With only a handful of words he could virtually flay the skin from her bones.

Sex that good is rare. Just when had she forgotten how he felt about her? Just when had she forgotten that he thought of her as a gold-digging, lying cheat, who had taken advantage of him when he was vulnerable? Vulnerable. She studied Roel: a superb male animal in peak physical condition. A guy who looked at her with lust and cool mingled. A guy quite capable of having sex with her and then forgetting she existed. In short, someone likely to hurt her a good deal if she didn't watch out…

'This isn't going to happen ever again,' Hilary swore, spinning on her heel and heading for the door in a blind need to escape the scene of her own downfall.

'Not for the next twenty-four hours at least,' Roel conceded with velvet-smooth precision. 'I leave for Zurich this evening. I'll see you tomorrow evening.'

Hilary considered several counter-attacks of the don't-hurry-home variety before deciding that any such response would be less than impressive after the mortifying way she had behaved with him. In chagrined silence she left his office. A knot of executive types wearing perplexed expressions was waiting outside. Everybody backed away to let her pass. Convinced that what she had been doing was somehow written on her pink-cheeked face, she walked to the lift at speed.

He had somehow discovered the magic combination that transformed her into a woman who acted like a slut. For that alone, she should hate him, she told herself. But at that point she recalled Roel's own initial reactions in the aftermath of their intimacy. He had been knocked off balance by the passion that had betrayed them both. He had also informed her that she was banned from his office. Banned as though she was possessed of such overpowering appeal that only a complete embargo on her presence could keep him on the sexual straight and narrow.

She tossed her head back. A very slight swing assailed her hips while a cheeky grin of one-upmanship dared to tug at the tight line of her compressed lips.

CHAPTER EIGHT

THE next day one-upmanship was not in Hilary's thoughts when she contemplated her breakfast with an appetite that had once again chosen to disappear. She was actually feeling quite nauseous. Not for the first time in recent days either, she reflected. Had she picked up some virus? But it was not as though she felt truly ill, more as though something was not quite right.

Only while she was considering that conundrum did it dawn on her that her body was behaving oddly in other ways as well. A quick calculation on her fingers suggested that her period was a few days over-due. She recounted, but accurate dates evaded her be-cause she had never bothered to keep a record of her cycle. She was getting her dates mixed up, she told herself. About there she froze on a very much belated acknowledgement that, from that very first night she had spent with Roel, she had done nothing whatso-ever to protect herself from becoming pregnant. And nor had he.

Everything that had happened with Roel had hap-pened so fast. Their intimacy had not been a pre-planned event. At no stage had she even thought of the risk that she might conceive a child. Had Roel been as thoughtless as she had been? Or had he as-sumed that she was taking the contraceptive pill? For goodness' sake, why was she working herself up into such a state?

The previous month she had only shared Roel's bed for a week. How likely was it that she could have conceived in so short a space of time? Hadn't she read a newspaper article about falling fertility rates? Most probably stress had upset her menstrual cycle and that very disruption was throwing her whole system out of sync and making her feel unwell. She would wait a few days and if she were still concerned she would have a pregnancy test. In the meantime it would be madness for her to start fretting herself into a panic over something that might never happen.

Umberto brought her a phone. It was Roel.

'I meant to call you last night but the meeting went on too late,' he asserted.

His dark, deep drawl sounded wonderful on the phone line and she was furious with herself for noticing that. 'Don't worry about it. I wasn't expecting to hear from you.'

'We're attending a party tonight, *cara*.'

'Oh, so I get a night out for good behaviour,' she sniped.

'And a night in for bad. No prizes for guessing which I would prefer,' he incised smoothly. 'I'm no party animal.'

While she dressed that evening she waited with bated breath for the communicating door between their bedrooms to open. Sheathed in a green evening dress that bared her shoulders and accentuated the creamy perfection of her pale skin, she finally descended the stairs.

Roel strolled out into the hall below her. Heavily lidded dark-as-night eyes scanned her and glittered gold with appreciation. 'You look good.'

Madly conscious of his scrutiny, she turned pink. 'No need to sound so surprised.'

'It crossed my mind that you might try to score points by opting to wear something totally inappropriate,' Roel admitted.

'I wouldn't be that childish.' She cleared her throat. 'I put the wedding ring back on…by the way.'

'Why not? You worked hard enough for it,' Roel derided with silken cool.

Her face flamed as though he had slapped her. 'When you speak to me like that I hate you!'

Roel vented a jeering laugh. 'It's traditional for hatred to blossom between married couples in my family.'

'Your mother fell for someone else. That didn't mean she hated your father—'

'Didn't it? She was in love with that same man when she married my father. My father's love turned to hate when he realised the truth.'

Hilary winced. 'Why on earth did she marry him?'

'Money,' Roel said succinctly, tucking her into the limousine waiting outside the house. 'My grandmother was equally rapacious but more moral. She gave my grandfather, Clemente, one child and then informed him that her duty was done. Although they remained below the same roof until her death, they never lived as man and wife again.'

'It seems wrong that your mother married your father when she loved another man. But maybe there were pressures on her that you don't know about or maybe she even believed that she was doing the *right* thing and would learn to love your father,' Hilary contended, keen to encourage him to be less judgemental when it came to other people's mistakes.

'That possibility had never occurred to me,' Roel said very drily. 'Do you suppose that she gave birth to me in the hope that she might learn to love me too?'

Hilary blenched at the cutting note of ridicule in that suggestion. 'I was only trying to say that there are two sides to any unhappy marriage and there might have been extenuating circumstances...I was trying to comfort you.'

'But I don't need comfort.' Bold, bronzed face taut, Roel spoke with acid clarity. 'I don't even remember my mother. She died before I was four years old.'

'How?'

Roel shrugged. 'She drowned.'

'I'm sorry you never had the chance to know her. Yes, I know you think I'm very sentimental,' she conceded. 'But if you only knew how *much* I would give to have my mother back to talk to for just five minutes...I would do just about anything for that chance—'

'If you can't persuade your heart to bleed in silence,' Roel interrupted with icy derision, 'I'll attend the party on my own.'

'I think that would be the best idea,' Hilary retorted a little unevenly because her eyes were glimmering with tears and her throat was closing over. 'I don't think I want to spend one more second in the company of someone as unfeeling as you are!'

'We're almost at the airport. Calm down. You're too emotional—'

'Not an affliction likely to attack you, is it?' Hilary slashed back at him shakily. 'I'm not ashamed of my emotions.'

'I am not asking you to be ashamed, merely to keep them in check,' Roel decreed with immoveable cool.

But Hilary was finding it quite impossible to control the number of powerful emotions swilling about inside her. 'I loved my parents very much and I still miss them terribly. They taught me to think the best of everybody and even though I soon learned that the world isn't always that nice a place—'

'Who taught you that lesson?'

'My father's cousin, Mandy. The minute she knew our parents were dead she went into action. She convinced Social Services that she was a fit and proper person to take responsibility for raising Emma. I was considered too young and I was terrified that my sister and I would be parted. Mandy moved us all into a big rented house…' Hilary recalled painfully.

'*And?*' Roel prompted.

'Mandy and her boyfriend then fleeced us out of every penny they could lay their hands on. She got control of the money my parents had left. There wasn't a lot but there would've been enough to keep Emma and I comfortable for a few years. When there was nothing more left to steal or sell, she just walked out one day and never came back.'

'I assume you called in the police. Misuse of funds in a situation of that nature is a crime.'

'The money was gone and nothing was going to bring it back. I had more important things to worry about—like finding somewhere cheaper to live and looking after my sister,' Hilary countered defensively.

In an unexpected gesture of sympathy, Roel closed his hand over her clenched fingers. 'You trusted Mandy because she was related to you. Her betrayal must have come as a considerable shock.'

'Yeah…' She was dismayed to realise that, far from receding, that dangerous and unfamiliar urge to burst into floods of tears was merely growing stronger.

'When I had amnesia, I had no choice but to trust you,' Roel murmured with husky bite, dark golden eyes resting on her with punitive force. 'I believed you were my wife—'

Hilary yanked her hand free of his grip with positive violence. 'You don't need to say any more…I've got the message. But all I did was try and act like your wife. I did not go to bed with you with any ulterior motive, nor do I have any intention of trying to make money out of our marriage!'

'Only time will prove the truth of that claim.'

'Look, what's your problem? You're an incredibly good-looking, sexy bloke yet you seem to find it impossible to accept that any woman could want you just for yourself!' Hilary slammed back at him chokily.

'Or for my body,' Roel countered in a tone smoother than silk.

With a suddenness that shook her, Hilary lost her head in an explosion of rage she could not control. 'You see, that's just one of those things I can't stand about you. You always have to have the last word and it's always a smart-ass remark. You're so convinced that you never do anything wrong that you blame me for everything. If the sky fell down on us right this minute, you'd say it was my fault!'

'Sì…' Roel responded, impervious to attack, a bright glitter in his intent scrutiny. 'Screaming has been known to cause avalanches.'

Hilary breathed in so deep in an effort to restrain

herself that she was honestly afraid she might burst. But she was seeing his extravagantly handsome features through a mist of red. In that brief interim in hostilities, the chauffeur swept open the door.

'I just want you to know that I *hate* you!' Hilary was reduced to hissing shrewishly at him as he settled into the seat beside hers on the helicopter.

He meshed long brown fingers into her hair and held her still for the descending force of his mouth. She fell into that kiss much as if she had charged full tilt off a precipice. Down and down and down she went into the hot, wild, honeyed excitement of it. The stinging electrical charge of his seething sensuality took her prisoner and she revelled in every moment of his unleashed passion.

He drew back an inch, fierce golden eyes blazing over her. 'We'll stay only forty minutes at the party.'

She was out of breath and stunned by the frightening intensity of her own emotions. She saw inside herself, understood why she had been fighting with him and struggling to hold him at a distance. He had so much power to hurt her and hurt her he would while she still loved him. 'Roel...'

'You make me burn for you...I barely slept a night through while you were in London. But now you're mine again and you will *stay* mine until I decide otherwise, *bella mia*.'

The helicopter delivered them to a huge, opulent yacht where they were greeted by their hosts like visiting royalty. Hilary was in a daze. All she was really conscious of was Roel, his big powerful frame taut and restless by her side, the possessive masculine arm anchored to her spine. Good manners took him from her when his host urged him over to meet an old friend.

Hilary clutched her untouched glass of wine. The music and the chattering voices seemed to be crowding in on her. Her hostess introduced a constant procession of strange faces to her. The bright dresses of the women and the glitter of their fabulous jewellery blurred in her gaze and she blinked. The slight motion of the yacht beneath her did not help. Clammy heat assailed her and she felt horribly sick and dizzy. Even as she turned in desperation to look for a seat it was too late and she slid down on the deck in a dead faint.

When she recovered consciousness, Roel was staring down at her with cloaked dark eyes. 'Take it easy, *cara*. I'm taking you home.'

Lashes fluttering down again, she offered up a silent prayer that the nausea would evaporate. He lifted her up into his arms, exchanged a brief dialogue with their concerned hosts and carried her back up to the upper deck to board the helicopter again.

'I don't think I've ever seen a more immediate or magical performance,' Roel informed her with mocking appreciation once the craft was airborne.

Belatedly she recalled his assertion that he was prepared to spend less than an hour at the party and only then appreciated that he honestly believed she had staged a fake collapse to please him and achieve an even earlier departure. The wheels and dips of the flight did nothing to settle her uneasy tummy and conversation was beyond her. At the back of her mind lurked worrying questions that increased her tension. Why had she fainted? She had never fainted in her life before, but she remembered Pippa telling her that dizzy spells were common in early pregnancy.

Vaulting off the helicopter as soon as it had landed, Roel swung back to assist her. 'That was a most impressive faint.' A wickedly sensual smile illuminated his lean dark features. 'For a moment, even I thought it was for real.'

'It was…I think I got seasick,' Hilary mumbled, leaning against him because her legs still felt distinctly untrustworthy in the support department.

'*Seasick?*' Roel exclaimed.

'I still don't feel so great,' Hilary added apologetically.

Roel groaned and bent down to lift her again. 'Seasick,' he breathed in wonderment. 'You were only on board fifteen minutes.'

An hour later she was lying in bed, circumspectly clad in a nightdress. Roel was poised by the foot of the bed and surveying her with keen attention. 'I don't want to lie here like a corpse,' she was protesting by then. 'I feel great now.'

'Healthy people don't faint,' Roel drawled in a censorious tone as if it were something she could have helped. 'If the doctor says it's OK, you can get up again.'

'Doctor…what doctor?' she gasped.

A knock sounded on the door. 'That should be her now. I called her from the limo to request a home visit.'

In sheer fright, Hilary sat up. 'I don't want to see a doctor…for goodness' sake, I don't need to!'

'Let me be the judge of that—'

'What's it got to do with you?'

'I'm your husband. I'm responsible for your well-being,' Roel imparted grittily. 'Even if you are ungrateful for my concern.'

Shame and embarrassment silenced Hilary. He opened the door to an older woman with greying dark hair swept up in a no-nonsense style.

'I'd like to see the doctor alone,' Hilary announced when Roel betrayed a nerve-racking reluctance to leave the bedroom.

She answered the doctor's questions honestly and submitted to an examination. Afterwards, the woman smiled. 'I think you already suspect the cause. You're pregnant.'

Hilary lost colour because all she could think of at that instant was how unwelcome such an announcement would be to Roel. 'Are you sure?'

The older woman nodded. 'Certain signs are unmistakable.'

'I don't want to tell my husband yet,' Hilary confided.

Her body had shocked her. She was going to have Roel's baby. Maybe a little boy with black hair and an irresistible smile or a minx of a little girl with glorious tigerish eyes and a belief that she ruled the world. Yes, she was going to have Roel's baby and, unless she was very much mistaken, he would hate her for it.

When Roel entered the room she couldn't look at him and she scrambled out of bed. 'What are you doing?' he demanded.

'I was a little bit seasick and now I'm fine and I'm getting dressed.'

Roel scooped her up mid-step and deposited her back on the bed. 'No. The doctor said you needed a sensible meal and plenty of sleep and I intend to ensure that you follow her advice.'

'Benevolence doesn't suit you,' she told him waspishly while he stood over her to watch her eat the delicious food, which had been brought to her on a tray embellished with flowers.

Roel sent her a languorous smile that made her heartbeat quicken and her tummy flip. 'I'm only thinking of my own needs.'

'Oh, really?'

'You'll have to be one hundred per cent fit to meet my expectations over the next few days. I've decided to take a break—'

'But you don't take breaks—'

'Give me you and a bed…and a PC connection and I can take a break.'

Hilary went pink to the roots of her hair.

'I shall get you out from under my skin or die in the attempt, *cara*,' Roel murmured huskily.

'Then what?'

In the silence that fell she was too enervated even to take the breath she needed lest it somehow obscured his answer.

'I fly you home and return to my free and uncomplicated former life as a single male.'

It took immense courage but she did not flinch at that comeback. 'So why wait? Why not do that now?'

'Right now I'm still enjoying you. You're different from my usual lovers.'

'Does how I feel come into this in any way?' Hilary snapped.

'I make you feel *incredible* and you know it,' Roel reminded her with merciless cool and the cruel intimacy of a lover, well aware of his own ability to turn her inside out and upside down with sheer longing.

Hilary subsided back into the pillows and closed her mortified eyes. Sometimes forbearance was the better part of valour, she reminded herself. Sometimes there was nothing wrong with just going with the flow. He might never need to know that she had conceived his child. Did she really *have* to tell him? When they parted, she would never see him again. She wanted their baby so much and she had loads of love to give. She was prepared to work incredibly hard to give their child a decent home. How could she be such a coward that she was already trying to excuse herself for not immediately telling Roel that she had fallen pregnant?

'I told you I didn't want anything,' Hilary whispered urgently under her breath the instant the unctuous salesman moved out of hearing. 'What are we doing in here?'

Roel dealt her a look of warm amusement. 'You have no jewellery. It's time I bought you some.'

Hilary stretched up on tiptoe to murmur with forced amusement, 'It's not wise to take the mistress idea out of the bedroom...the joke wears thin—'

'This time the joke's on me. No decent gold-digger would miss out on an opportunity of this magnitude.' As Hilary flinched in surprise and pain her eyes flew wide and darted up to lodge on his lean dark chiselled features. He curved an imprisoning arm round her slight, taut figure to prevent her from pulling back from him. 'Think about what I just said,' he urged in a husky tone of intimacy. 'In fact maybe you should be capturing this on film. I'm admitting that I misjudged your motives four years ago...'

Hilary snatched in a stark breath. 'Are you serious?'

'Never more so.' Taking advantage of her shock,

Roel manoeuvred her down onto the elegant stool by the counter. 'Some sad individuals say sorry with flowers—'

'Is that a fact?' she said breathlessly, hardly able to think straight because he had plunged her from hurt straight into a disconcerted state of relief and happiness.

'Some never say sorry at all and some will even buy you diamonds in the hope that you will not expect any action that could be interpreted as grovelling.'

Her easy smile broke out like the sun at dawn and she almost laughed out loud, for she had never forgotten him saying that grovelling was only for peasants.

An hour later, when they had returned to the villa, she wandered out onto the terrace where he was enjoying a drink. A giant ancient fig tree provided shelter from the sultry heat of the Sardinian sun. Even late afternoon, it was very hot. Lush planted terraces and steps ran down the steep hillside to the private beach below.

'It obviously pays to catch you out,' she teased Roel, angling up her wrist so that the platinum watch glittered in the arrow of light breaking through the leafy canopy above her. And all the while she was doing that she was still watching Roel, luxuriating in his proximity, his bold, uncompromising masculinity and even that fierce will of his, which she had dared to cross in that exclusive jewellery store.

As always attuned to her scrutiny, Roel elevated an ebony brow, his brilliant dark eyes full of reproof for she had been adamant about accepting only that one gift. 'I wanted to cover you in diamonds.'

'I'd have looked downright silly,' she quipped.

'Naked you would have looked like a pagan goddess, *bella mia*.'

Her tummy flipped. It took Roel to imagine her as nobody else ever would. Self-conscious beneath his molten appraisal, she muttered unevenly, 'You still haven't explained why you changed your mind about me being greedy for money?'

His lean, strong face tensed. 'When you claimed in London that you'd paid most of the cash settlement I gave you back into the account from which you originally received it, I didn't believe you. But I had it checked out. That money has been lying unacknowledged in that account for well over three years—'

'But what happened to the letter I wrote to Paul Correro?'

'It never arrived. Around that time he moved into new legal offices. Your letter would have been sent to his old address and it must have gone astray. Paul is very upset about all this.' His handsome mouth compressed in acknowledgement. 'He knows he is the broken link in a chain, which has led to much misunderstanding between us.'

Hilary was grateful that the subject of that cash settlement could finally be freely discussed. 'I never meant to take money from you but I did, so you can hardly blame him for having a low opinion of me—'

'He had no right to make that judgement—'

A pained light had entered Hilary's unguarded gaze for she was tempted to point out that Paul Correro had simply taken his lofty air of disapproval from Roel himself. 'I'd like to explain a couple of things. When we first met, Emma and I were living in a rough area and her friends were kids who thought it was fun to shoplift. She was skipping school and I was having trouble controlling her.'

Roel was listening with grave attention. 'I had no idea your home life was that grim. You always seemed so cheerful.'

'A long face doesn't change anything for the better. Your money gave us a new start. I rented the flat, opened up the salon and got Emma into another school. All the problems we were having vanished one by one,' Hilary explained. 'I didn't have to work evenings any more, so she had to stay home and she studied. The next year she won her scholarship and she has never looked back since.'

'You should be proud of yourself. I wish you had been more frank with me at the time—'

As she connected with his stunning golden gaze Hilary's mouth ran dry and she looked away. 'In those days, you didn't want to know.'

'I wouldn't allow myself to get to know you and you paid the price for that. But that was then and this is now...' Enclosing her hand in his, Roel pressed a slow, burning, sensual kiss to her palm.

She quivered, legs trembling, heat surging between her slender thighs. At a leisurely pace he undid her wrap top and flicked loose the clasp on the silk bra she wore beneath.

'It's broad daylight...' she muttered.

'You shock so easily,' Roel savoured, pressing her back against the sun-warmed wall and peeling off her sarong skirt. 'Relax...I will do everything.'

And, shamelessly, she let him. There against the worn stone wall he stripped her naked. She was bo-neless, ready for him even before he scored expert fingers through the silvery blonde curls crowning her feminine mound to tease the swollen, sensitive, secret flesh below. He probed her passion-moistened depths with a carnal skill that made her sob out loud against her own fierce and unbearable longing.

'Don't stop…' she cried hoarsely.

'I love it when you're out of control. It makes me want to drive you even wilder.' Roel flipped her round and bent her over the wall, lifting her up to penetrate her with his hard male heat. Shock and overwhelming delight made her dizzy. He filled her to the hilt. She couldn't breathe for excitement. Sensation made her forget everything but the fierce, desperately rousing surge of his demanding body into hers. His animal passion sent her flying into glorious frenzy of release.

In the aftermath, he gathered her limp body up into his arms and carried her into the shuttered cool of the bedroom. He discarded his own clothes. All rippling muscle and damp bronzed skin, he was magnificent. Coming down on the bed, he drew her back into his arms and smiled with slumberous satisfaction and approval down at her. She wanted to cry with love for him. She wanted that sweet moment of silent intimacy to last for ever. He smoothed her hair out of her eyes, kissed her, held her close and she felt as frantic as though she were trying to live her whole life out in those minutes when she was at her happiest.

'I adore your breasts,' Roel confided lazily, lifting her up to arrange her astride him and reaching up to cup the pert, firm mounds with unashamed masculine appreciation. 'I swear they've got fuller since the first time we made love.'

Hilary lowered her lashes to hide the panic in her eyes.

'Not that I'm complaining, you understand,' Roel breathed huskily. 'I've noticed what a pushover you are for Swiss chocolate…'

He thought she was putting on the beef because she was stuffing herself with chocolate drinks! She rolled off him in haste.

Roel groaned out loud and tugged her back to him by dint of his greatly superior strength. 'Don't be so touchy. You have a to-die-for shape. Angels in heaven would fight over you and I shall revel in keeping you stocked up with chocolate,' he imparted. 'It's very refreshing to be with a woman who eats whatever she feels like.'

So not only did he think she was overweight, but also a greedy pig into the bargain, Hilary thought crazily. If only that were true…if only an over-indulgence in chocolate *were* responsible for the fact that her bosom had already jumped an entire cup size!

'I'm going for a shower,' she muttered, yanking herself free of his loosened hold and scrambling off the bed.

'How the hell can you suffer from such low self-esteem?' Roel sat up to demand with very male frustration.

'I saw Celine…beside her, I'd probably look as heavenly in shape as Humpty Dumpty!' Hilary fielded chokily.

Anger brightening his spectacular gaze, Roel sprang out of bed. '*Che idea!* Celine answered my needs…but you arouse them. I can't keep my hands off you for longer than an hour. I've even taken time out from the bank to be with you.'

Her eyelids were gritty with unshed tears. 'That's just sex,' she accused.

A ferocious silence fell and she waited and she prayed for him to break that silence with even a single word of disagreement.

Roel stared back at her with stony, stubborn intensity, black-lashed brilliant dark eyes unreadable, his long, lean, powerful frame still as a predator ready to fend off attack.

Her throat ached so much with disappointment that it really hurt. He had not contradicted her. She should have known better than to hope that he would. With a brittle throwaway smile designed to persuade him that a purely physical relationship was fine by her, she disappeared into the bathroom and locked the door behind her.

She switched on the shower. Tears were rolling down her cheeks. She choked back her sobs. Sex was all she had ever had to offer him and nobody could say he had not taken full advantage of her willingness. Or that she had any grounds for complaint. It was a week since he had brought her to Sardinia, to this fantastic coastal villa where they enjoyed complete seclusion and sheer, unvarnished luxury.

For seven days they had been inseparable. There had been picnics on the beach, moonlight swims, late-night romantic dinners, languorous siestas in the heat of the day and long discussions about all sorts of subjects on which they rarely ever agreed. He was incredibly stimulating company and wonderfully entertaining. When he needed to work for an hour or two, she had taken to curling up nearby with a magazine and keeping him company. For her it had been a time of idyllic happiness but also a challenging time while she'd slowly struggled to come to terms with the reality that she was carrying his baby.

Physically she was feeling terrific. But then she had been careful about what she ate and now rested whenever she felt tired. Roel had teased her about her slothful ways but her body had rewarded her newly learnt caution. The nausea had been less of a problem and she had only once felt light-headed when she stood up too fast. Yet already her body was changing to a degree where even Roel had noticed that her breasts were bigger. In fact her bras were becoming uncomfortably tight. Keeping her condition a secret would not be an option for much longer. Nevertheless she was filled with sick dread at the prospect of having to tell Roel that she had conceived.

This time around with him she had been determined not to build fantasy castles in the air. She had faced everything in their relationship as it was and not as she would have liked it to be. Every morning, before she got around to kissing him awake in the variety of imaginative ways that he most liked, she had duly reminded herself of certain hard facts…

He was not in love with her. He was in lust and it was lust that made him an insatiable lover. That he could spend hours just talking to her, that he could also be amazingly tender and amusing and caring, was irrelevant. After all, he was a hugely sophisticated guy and it was impossible to imagine him being guilty of coarse or ignorant behaviour. She was not his wife in the truest sense of the word because he had once given her a fee to go through that wedding ceremony with him. She was the wife he had bought, not the wife he might have chosen.

Furthermore she would never fit the mould of the perfect partner whom he would eventually pick. She matched none of his instinctive preferences…yes, one by one, she had weaselled those preferences out of him without him even realising just how much information he was revealing. He liked leggy brunettes and his last mistress had also been terrifyingly beautiful. He thought background and breeding were important. He believed a university education was crucial. She failed on every count. She was not and never could be a wife whom he might want to keep.

On those grounds, the news that she was expecting his baby was likely to strike Roel as a total disaster. That was why she had been so reluctant to tell him. That was why she had prevaricated for seven entire days and lived every precious moment as though it might be the last she ever spent with him. But, in all fairness to him, it was time she spoke up.

She donned peacock-blue silk trousers with an artfully simple embroidered matching top. The shade accentuated the colour of her eyes. Only a month earlier she had worn a lot more make-up but now she applied cosmetics with a much lighter hand. Roel had introduced her to a different world and she had naturally studied the women within those exclusive circles. Always observant and quick to learn, she had soon recognised how more subtle effects could enhance her appearance. But she was growing out her short, spiky hairstyle purely for Roel's benefit…

'It's the most fantastic colour,' he had intoned with flattering appreciation, 'but I want more of it, *lots* more of it! I want to see your hair rippling down your back like a fantastic sheet of silver, *bella mia*.'

'But it would take for ever even for it to grow down to my shoulders,' Hilary had complained.

'I'll wait…I can be very patient when I want something.'

And, solely to please him, she had promised not to cut her hair short again. She had not allowed herself to wonder how many inches her spiky tresses might get to grow before how she wore them became a matter of the most complete indifference to him.

The table was set for dinner on the terrace. It was very beautiful. Coloured glass lanterns hung in the branches of the fig tree and candles glittered in the midst of crystal glasses and gilded bone china. At a lower level and screened by vegetation she could just see a reflective glimmer of the swimming pool in the moonlight.

It was Roel's villa. Sometimes he only visited it once a year and some years not even that. He owned an enormous amount of property round the world. He did not like hotels. Even here, in one of the more remote locations on the island, Roel received only the best service and a chef was still on hand to produce the most superb meals. Within the cocoon of Roel's almost unimaginable wealth he took for granted a level of freedom and comfort that other people could only dream about and envy. He had complete control. How was he likely to react to what she had to tell him? To a situation that she could not allow him to control? Her soft mouth quivered with the tempestuous emotion she was fighting to repress.

Roel strode out to join her. 'Turn round,' he invited her huskily.

A little stiffly, she obliged.

'You look delectable…I could devour you like an animal,' he confessed with a frankness that sent a piercing shard of shameful excitement flaring through her taut figure. 'Think yourself lucky if I can restrain myself to the end of our meal.'

In strained silence she moistened her bone-dry mouth with a hasty sip of mineral water.

Keen dark golden eyes rested on her and his beautiful mouth took on a humorous quirk. 'Humpty Dumpty…I don't think so,' he pronounced.

A miserable flush lit her fair skin. She wanted to seal her lips closed, rush into his arms and hug him tight, hold onto the happiness he had given her.

'You've been very moody the past few days,' Roel continued.

Disconcerted, she shot him a glance. 'Er…I—'

'One minute you're smiling like mad and the next you're way down deep in the doldrums and all weepy,' Roel slotted in. 'That's not your nature, so I assume it's PMT.'

Hilary flinched and then braced herself to stand as rigid as a stick of rock. 'I have something to tell you,' she said starkly.

CHAPTER NINE

A SUDDEN irreverent smile slashed Roel's extraordinarily handsome features. 'Don't take this as a criticism. As a pragmatic male, I find your natural flair for drama fascinating,' he assured her in his dark deep drawl. 'But may we eat first? I have to confess that I'm very hungry.'

Nervous as a cat on hot bricks, Hilary nibbled at the soft underside of her lower lip. His raw charisma, his vast confidence that she could have nothing of any great import to confide, knocked her off balance. She sank down at the table. By the time the main course had been served, her contribution to the conversation had sunk to the level of monosyllabic responses.

'When you go this quiet, it worries me,' Roel commented.

'Sometimes I talk too much,' she said uncomfortably.

'But I'm so accustomed to it now that I like it, *cara mia*.'

Roel stroked a blunt forefinger down over her clenched fingers where they rested on the pristine table cloth. 'Obviously I miscalculated when I implied that you couldn't have anything that couldn't stand a rain check to tell me.'

'Yes…' Hilary swallowed hard. 'But it's not something you could have guessed and I—'

His intent gaze flashed a sudden stormy gold. 'Did

you sleep with that guy I surprised on your doorstep in London?'

That icy demand shook her. 'Gareth? No...no, of course not!'

'Just checking out my worst case scenario,' Roel told her, deadpan.

'Will you hear me out before you say anything?' Hilary pressed unevenly.

'I'm not in the habit of shouting people down.'

'Don't be angry with me...I know that's going to be hard but don't be angry with me,' she heard herself plead and she despised her own weakness. 'In one sense, we're both responsible.'

Hard jaw line clenching at that statement, Roel surveyed her with narrowed eyes. 'The point being? My patience has limits...'

'I'm...' She fiddled with the fork in her hand and put it down, her insides hollow with fear and lack of food for she had been unable to bring herself to eat a morsel. 'I've fallen pregnant...it happened the first week we were together.'

His natural colour ebbed from below his healthy olive skin, accentuating the slashing prominence of his superb bone structure.

'I know you've got to be shocked. I was shocked too,' she admitted tightly.

Shimmering golden eyes executed a search and destroy mission over her shrinking figure. In one powerfully revealing motion, Roel thrust back his chair and sprang upright. He strode over to the wall like a tiger on the prowl and stood looking out into the night. In the terrible silence, the surge of the surf on the beach sounded eerily loud.

Awkwardly she cleared her throat. 'I never dreamt

that I would end up in bed with you and, when it happened, I didn't even think about contraception. There was so much else going on and I *knew* I shouldn't have let you make love to me and I felt so guilty…all those things got in the way.'

His back was still turned to her. She longed for him to turn round. His broad shoulders were rigid with tension, corded muscle visible beneath the thin, expensive fabric of his black short-sleeved shirt.

'I know you're annoyed about this.' She pleated her fingers together in a strained gesture. 'That's OK…that's understandable. You weren't expecting this situation to develop. But I wasn't either. I couldn't cope with a termination though, so let's not discuss that…'

In receipt of that hoarse plea for his understanding on that score, Roel swung round and directed a bleak look at her from impassive eyes so dark they chilled her to the marrow.

'I know…I know. Maybe you didn't even *want* to discuss that option. But it's easier if I say now that this may not be a planned baby but I-I'll make it welcome all the same,' she stammered. 'Although, right now, I just feel scared and overwhelmed by all this.'

Roel helped himself to a very stiff whisky and tossed it back in one unappreciative gulp.

Her taut face stamped with apprehension, Hilary rose from behind the table and moved on stiff legs to the middle of the terrace. 'Please say something…'

'You're now the future mother of my child.' The insolent edge to his intonation somehow made the label sound like a freezingly polite term of abuse and she stiffened and paled. 'I have to be very careful what I say to you. A pregnant wife has many rights and not the least is civilised consideration for her condition. How long have you known?'

'Since you called in that nice doctor after I fainted.'

Roel bit out a harsh laugh. '*That* long? How did you manage to keep your promising announcement under wraps all of this week?'

'Easily…if I could have run away from it, I would've,' she confided half under her breath. 'I didn't…*don't* want to lose you—'

Hard dark eyes assailed hers with merciless force. 'You never had me…except in the most basic way.'

'I know,' she whispered jaggedly. 'But this is still about to wreck what we have.'

'Don't presume to know what I think or I feel. Or what I intend to do next,' Roel advised her grimly.

'You're free to tell me what you're thinking. I won't take offence.' She was desperate to bridge the chasm that had opened up between them and if the truth hurt, so be it.

His lean, intelligent face hardened. '*Bene*…very well. Why should I be surprised by your achievement? The babies in the Sabatino family have always come with a very large price label attached.'

'Not our baby…' Hilary told him with fierce conviction.

Ruthless cynicism laced the derisive light in his keen gaze. He strode past her as if she weren't there and went indoors. After a disconcerted pause she chased after him and caught up with him in the main hall as he was leaving the villa.

'Not our baby,' she said again and her voice might have quivered but her eyes were resolute and she frowned. 'Are you going out?'

Roel dealt her a hard mocking look. 'What do you think?'

'Where are you going?'

'That's my business.'

Long after his departure, she was still hovering in the hall hugging herself as if she were cold. Eventually she pulled herself together and walked back out to the terrace. The staff had already cleared the table. She thought of the tiny life in her womb and wondered if it was suffering because she hadn't eaten and her eyes stung like mad. She ordered toast and a chocolate drink for supper.

And all the time she was trying not to dwell on how Roel had behaved. As if he utterly despised her. As if she was beneath contempt. As if she had got pregnant deliberately and planned to sell her baby to him for the highest possible price. He had hurt her but she still felt that it was better that he had voiced what he was feeling. But she wished he had not gone out. An hour after his departure, she called him on his mobile phone.

'Are you coming home soon?' she asked with fake cheer.

'I'm not coming *home* at all,' Roel breathed icily.

'Before you make your mind up about that,' Hilary muttered anxiously, 'I should warn you that if you stay out all night I'll be very unhappy about it. I don't think I could just sit here waiting either. I'd be so worried I'd have to come and look for you—'

'We are not having this conversation.' He killed the call.

Half an hour later, bolstered by her toast, she called him back. When he answered she heard a soft femi-nine giggle somewhere close by and her heart sank to her toes. 'Are you with a woman?' she demanded sickly.

'If you phone again, I won't answer.'

'I think we're worth fighting for but I couldn't forgive infidelity…' she warned him shakily, her throat thick with tears.

'Emotional blackmail doesn't work with me.'

'What about hysterics? Look, I know I sound like a maniac but all I want is for you to come back here and talk.'

'But I don't want to and you will not make me do what I don't want to do.'

It was one in the morning when Roel appeared in the bedroom doorway. She was lying awake in the moonlight and she had left the door wide so that she could listen out for his return. Sitting up with a jerk, she switched on the bedside lamps. Black hair tousled, dark stubble outlining his obdurate jaw line, Roel stared across the depth of the room at her. Without hesitation, she scrambled off the bed and raced over to hurl herself at him. He had come back. That was all she cared about at that instant.

'No…' That single word was very decisive, very, very unyielding. He set her back from him with cool hands.

She fell back a step, horribly crushed by that rejection, suddenly conscious that with her mussed hair and red swollen eyes she had to look like hell. She was also fearfully aware of the weak part of her willing to do or say anything to hold onto him. But she knew that wouldn't work. If she crawled, Roel would walk right over the top of her and despise her even more.

'I've reached certain decisions,' Roel delivered.

'It takes two people to make a decision in a marriage,' Hilary dared.

'Not when only *one* of them is in the wrong,' Roel splintered back at her without hesitation.

Hilary sucked in a slow deep breath. If she fought with him, he would only get angrier. It wouldn't hurt her to stand a little humble pie while emotions got the chance to simmer down.

'I want you to have a medical examination so that the relevant dates can be checked. Before the baby is born I want to be as certain as I can be that it's mine,' Roel drawled with no expression at all.

Her face pinching tight with pained mortification, she backed away from him. 'You have doubts?' she whispered and she was appalled that he could even suspect that someone else might have fathered the child she carried.

'Some women would kill for a tiny percentage cut of what that baby will be worth to you in financial terms,' Roel contended.

'Oh...I don't think any woman would kill to be me just at this moment,' Hilary mumbled unevenly because, instead of returning to talk, he had returned to annihilate her hopes.

'Naturally I'll have DNA testing carried out as a final check after the birth,' Roel continued as if she hadn't spoken. 'I'm aware that you could have conceived during those two weeks you spent back in London. I think it's unlikely but I'd be foolish not to seek full confirmation.'

'Yeah...' A shadowy attempt at a smile briefly skimmed her tense mouth. 'Why hesitate when you've got yet another golden opportunity to humiliate me?'

'What did you expect? Approval? I refuse to believe that this pregnancy is an accidental development.' Scornful golden eyes settled on her. 'After all, conceiving my child ensures that you will live in luxury for the rest of your life.'

'You're not being fair to me. If you don't have any faith at all in me, how can I ever hope to prove that you've got me wrong?' Hilary slung at him in growing distress.

'But I *haven't* got you wrong—'

'Only today you were telling me that you accepted that I was never a gold-digger—'

'Before the latest revelation persuaded me otherwise—'

'How could I possibly have known that I would fall pregnant after one week with you?' she argued passionately. 'This is not how I would have chosen to have my first child. Why would I want to curse my baby with a reluctant father who hates me?'

'I'm not reluctant and I don't hate you—'

Hilary threw up her hands in frustration. 'All your anger stems back to the fact that when you had amnesia I kept you in the dark about our marriage—'

'You lied to me over and over again—'

'I didn't think I was doing any harm...so I got a bit carried away, so I was living my dream—'

'Now you're *finally* telling me the truth,' Roel sliced in with derisive satisfaction. 'You were so seduced by my lifestyle you didn't care how low you had to sink to enjoy the benefits—'

Hilary vented a bitter little laugh. 'For your information my dream was a fairy-tale marriage with a guy who treated me like an equal...yeah, how pathetic of me to put you into a scenario like that! The guy who wouldn't even give me a date when I was begging for it! But then it was *my* fantasy and not yours, so I—'

'*Santo cielo!* You made me *live* your stupid fantasy,' Roel grated with raw accusation.

Hilary lifted her head high and her eyes shone bright as jewels. 'Oddly enough, you seemed perfectly happy living in my fantasy…'

Roel went as rigid as if she had hit him. She paled, defiance leaking from her. The silence simmered like poison on the boil. Black fury glittered in his ferocious gaze.

'Let's concentrate on the baby,' Roel said glacially.

With difficulty Hilary focused her weary mind back to the all-important task of dissuading Roel from his conviction that she had set out to become pregnant. 'Please listen to me. When I slept with you, I didn't consider consequences. I've never had to worry about birth control before. I was heedless and foolish but nothing worse.' She sent him a look of appeal. 'You didn't think either.'

His lean, strong face clenched in disagreement. 'That first night, I checked the cabinet by the bed for condoms,' he revealed drily. 'I have always visited my lovers in their homes to retain my privacy. But you were my wife. Understandably the absence of contraception in my bedroom encouraged me to assume that you were taking care of that requirement.'

'The idea of precautions didn't cross your mind after that?'

Roel elevated a sardonic ebony brow. 'Contraception was scarcely in the forefront of my concerns. I had amnesia and a wife who was a total stranger.'

'As I recall…you found that angle more of a turn-on than a problem,' Hilary dared to remind him, desperate to break through his polished shield of self-command and penetrate his reserve.

'I chose to trust you. That was a mistake and, like all my mistakes, I expect to pay for it,' Roel spelt out with brutal cool. 'But you have to live with me knowing you for exactly what you are. A little schemer who got into my bed to turn a substantial profit!'

'If you don't get out...' Hilary framed unsteadily, rage and self-loathing and pain combining into a combustible flame of wretchedness inside her, 'I'm going to scream at you like a fishwife and physically attack you!'

Treating her to a sizzling appraisal, Roel scooped her up into his arms before she could even guess his intention. 'Stop dramatising yourself—'

'Put me down!' she launched at him furiously.

'No. It's late. You look exhausted and you *should* be asleep—'

'I'll go to bed when I—'

'Why do you think I came back tonight?' Roel demanded with an icy clarity that made her stop struggling and go limp in his arms.

'I don't know...'

'You're my wife and you're carrying my child. I hope that, no matter how angry I am, I know better than to risk your health.'

Superior bastard...she hated him! She shut her wounded eyes tight. She wanted to scream at him but knew he would read loads and loads of clever things out of being screamed at. Quiet as a mouse, she let him settle her back into bed. He handled her as if she were a pane of glass with a hairline crack running through it. She remembered his wild, explosive desire out on the terrace only hours earlier and she almost wept: he had just covered her up as though she were his great-great-great-grandmother. For the first time he slept away from her and she felt that rejection like a knife in her breast. He wasn't just spelling out the reality that she had no emotional hold on him, he was putting her at a physical distance as well.

The next morning they flew back to Switzerland. An hour into the flight, she abandoned her proud attempt to pretend that she watching the film she had selected. Roel was working. She hovered within a couple of feet of him and he ignored her.

'OK…I've got the message,' she proclaimed shakily. 'You just wish I'd vanish like the evil fairy!'

Lean, dark face grim and impatient, Roel lodged unimpressed dark golden eyes on her.

Hilary planted her hands on her hips. 'Don't look at me like I'm an attention-seeking child,' she told him hotly. 'If I'm getting on your nerves to that extent, go ahead and divorce me!'

Roel rose upright, graceful as a prowling jungle predator, and towered over her in the most intimidating fashion. Dense black lashes lowered over his hard, glittering gaze. 'I was wondering how long it would take you to make that demand. Sorry to disappoint you, but you don't qualify for the get-out-of-gaol-free card yet, *cara*.'

'What's that supposed to mean?'

'No separation, no divorce. You're staying in Switzerland where I can watch over you.'

Hilary thought it was interesting that, no matter how greedy and wicked he was determined to believe she was, he could think of no greater punishment than keeping her in Switzerland with him. The ache in her heart subsided a little and a tiny charge of hope flared. Perhaps she had been guilty of expecting too much too soon from him.

'How do you really feel about the baby?' she plucked up the courage to finally ask.

'I was planning on one eventually,' Roel conceded grudgingly with the same amount of emotion as he might have expended when voicing a desire to acquire a new set of cuff-links. 'Now it's coming sooner rather than later. I'll adjust…I have no choice but to do so.'

Her delicate features tightened and her nails bit sharp crescents into her palms. She returned to her seat. She would give him time. He was very stubborn, very cynical in his suspicions. He needed more time. He needed her understanding. She loved him so much. He would come round, wouldn't he?

But to what extent would Roel ever come round to accepting Hilary Ross, hairdresser, as his wife? And how long would her tenure last? He seemed to think it was his bounden duty to keep an eye on her while she was carrying his baby but he could well be planning on divorcing her straight after the birth. For all she knew he had already worked out the legal ins and outs of such timing.

He had never accepted her as his wife. Could she blame him for that? He had never asked her to be his wife and live with him and he had certainly not invited her to conceive his baby! It was important that she faced facts and the facts were painful, she conceded miserably. Roel felt trapped. Roel preferred his freedom.

If she sunk her pride all over again and was truly humble until things settled down, what was the most

she could hope to receive from the guy she adored?
That he would bed her again when he felt like sex?
Throw her the odd piece of very expensive jewellery
when she performed really well between the sheets?
And would he always be rubbing her nose in her mistakes? Making her feel small and cheap and like nothing? Was she really prepared to let that happen?

CHAPTER TEN

THE following morning, Roel took Hilary to see a consultant gynaecologist.

Roel disconcerted Hilary by asking loads of complex questions. The gynaecologist was delighted to answer him with a great deal of scientific detail. Hilary felt like a womb on legs. She was hurt that Roel felt able to reveal his first show of interest in their baby to a third party but not to her. Then she wondered dismally if he had simply been putting on an act for the sake of appearances.

In the three endless days that followed, Hilary became more and more unhappy. Roel was heading in to the Sabatino Bank practically before the sun came up and returning late in the evening. He did not eat a single meal with her, nor was he making the smallest effort to ease the tension between them. But he phoned her twice a day to ask how she was. That seemed to be about as intimate as he was prepared to get for the communicating door between their bedrooms remained rigidly closed. His frigid politeness chilled her.

On the fourth morning she got up at the crack of dawn. After a sleepy shower and a hurried effort to make herself presentable without either looking suspiciously overdressed or unsuitably sexy, she hurried downstairs to the dining room to join Roel for breakfast.

Lean, strong face taut, Roel studied her with frowning force. 'What are you doing up at this hour?'

'I wanted to see you. It was either breakfast…or a forbidden interruption to your working day.' A determined smile on her soft tense mouth as she attempted to make that weak joke, she looked at him hopefully.

Stunning dark golden eyes rested on her kimono-style dressing gown and his wide, sensual mouth took on an almost infinitesimal curl. Made of the finest silk, the garment covered her from throat to toe with a modesty that he considered highly deceptive. Her tiny waist was defined not just by the wide sash but also by the glorious contrast of the burgeoning swell of her lush breasts above and the ripe sweet curve of her hips below. He set down his coffee cup with a jarring rattle. Hilary helped herself to toast from the buffet table, her heart pounding like a drum. She was tormentingly aware of his intent scrutiny and of the sizzling tension in the atmosphere.

'I…' The tip of her tongue snaked out in a nervous flicker to moisten her lips as she turned back to face him and mustered the courage to rise above her pride and not count the cost. 'I'll miss you—'

'*Dannazione!* I don't want to hear it!' Tossing aside his morning paper, Roel sprang upright. Scorching angry derision fired his scrutiny and she gazed back at him wide-eyed, her lips parted in complete disconcertion.

'I'm not falling for it. Not even if you clamber on the table and dance like Salome! Been there, done that, don't require the postcard as a reminder when we'll be inundated with christening mugs in a few months' time!' Roel launched at her with withering bite. 'When I want you, I'll let you know.'

Tears of angry humiliation prickled at the back of her eyes. She listened to the limo drive off. Right, well that was that, then. He could get stuffed, she thought in an agony of swelling emotion. He needn't think he could get away with treating her like some slut who would do anything to get him back into bed! She should never have accompanied him back from Sardinia. That had been a crucial miscalculation. He had made his contempt clear and she had been too much of a drip to accept that their marriage, such as it had been, was over.

But before she left Switzerland pride demanded that she clear her own name and made Roel see just how wrong he had been about her. Pacing up and down her bedroom, she decided that there was really only one way of achieving that end. She would have a proper legal agreement drawn up that would prove once and for all that she had no mercenary intentions. Furthermore she knew just the guy to approach. Paul Correro would be overjoyed to see her sign away all right to the Sabatino billions and she would leave Switzerland with her dignity intact.

When she arrived at the lawyer's smart offices later that morning, she was ushered straight in to his presence. She was surprised that Paul was able to see her immediately and initially taken aback when he greeted her with an anxious look and actually thanked her very much for coming.

'Anya wanted to visit you and Roel and apologise but I fouled up to such an extent with you that I thought it would be wiser to let the dust settle first,' the blonde man confessed heavily. 'I threatened you and I frightened you. Believe me, that is not how I usually treat women—'

'I'm sure it's not,' Hilary said soothingly.

'When Roel realised that it was my fault that you had disappeared into thin air, he hit the roof and I don't blame him—'

'That wasn't your fault—'

'Don't try to make me feel better,' Paul groaned. 'I interfered in something that I should have stayed well back from. In retrospect it was obvious that there was a whole dimension to your relationship with Roel that I knew nothing about. But I went galloping in arrogantly convinced I was coming to his rescue. Roel needing rescue?' He loosed an embarrassed laugh. 'As if…'

'Wires got crossed. That's all. It's all over and done with now. Actually I came to see you today about something entirely different,' Hilary confided, striving to mask her unhappiness with a façade of calm. 'I need a lawyer to write up some legal stuff for me and to do it fairly quickly.'

When she gave a brief outline of her requirements, Paul could not conceal his dismay. 'A document of that nature would present me with a conflict of interests. I can't represent you and Roel. You need independent legal advice.'

Stiff with discomfiture, Hilary got up from her chair. 'OK.'

'Off the record…' Paul Correro hesitated and then pressed on with open concern. 'As a friend, and I would hope that some day you will be able to regard me in that light, I would advise you against following this route. I'm very much afraid that Roel might misunderstand your motives and be hurt.'

On the drive back to the town house, Hilary conceded that Paul was a very nice bloke. He was the polar opposite of Roel and therefore totally incapable of appreciating how a male of Roel's ice-cold intellect and emotional reserve operated. No matter how hard she tried she could not think of Roel and the concept of hurt in the same statement. In her opinion, Roel had shown himself inviolable. She was the one who kept on getting hurt.

Now she was asking herself why she had decided to go to such elaborate lengths to disprove Roel's conviction that she was a gold-digger in the first place. Why did she still care? He didn't love her. He thought the very worst of her. Even the sight of her at his breakfast table offended him. It was hard to believe that just a few days ago she had been so happy with him. Even harder to accept that she had believed this was a rough patch that they could survive.

The trouble was that, when it came to Roel Sabatino, she had always been willing to settle for too little. And, deservedly, too little was what she had received. There came a time, though, when she had to be mature enough to stand up for herself, take account of her own needs and bow out of a destructive relationship.

Roel would never tell Emma the truth about their marriage. Indeed, she marvelled that she had ever swallowed that outrageous threat whole. Although he did his utmost to hide it, Roel was very honourable, but he would never parade that reality because he saw it as a weakness. Perhaps she had seized on that threat as an excuse to be with Roel when she'd been desperate to have that excuse. But now it was over and she was lifting her pride back out of the closet where she had hidden it. He was an unhealthy addiction and it was time she got over him.

The car phone buzzed. It was Roel and the very sound of his rich, dark, accented drawl was sufficient to tip her teeming emotions over the edge. 'Please don't ask me how I'm feeling because I know you don't really care,' she heard herself condemn. 'I'm leaving you and I hope that you and your precious money live happily ever after!'

She sent the phone crashing down and trembled, shaken by what had erupted from her own lips. But it was the truth and he had deserved to hear it. He had flung her love back in her teeth for the last time. She was going to pour all her love over their child instead. The phone buzzed. She ignored it. Her mobile phone sounded out its tune and she switched it off. There was nothing more to say.

Half an hour later she was in her bedroom packing when the door crashed back on its hinges and framed Roel. 'You *can't* leave…I can't go through that again!' he swore with vehement force.

Caught unprepared by that turbulent entrance that was so uncharacteristic of the calm, controlled male she knew, Hilary stared at him. He was ashen, his proud cheekbones tight with tension. Fierce dark eyes locked to her. 'Have you any idea what it was like for me the last time?' he demanded. 'Don't you know what I went through?'

Numb in the face of a display of more emotion than he had ever shown her he possessed, Hilary shook her head slowly in dumb negative.

'*Santo cielo!* That first week before I regained my memories just about killed me. One minute you were there and the next you were gone and I hadn't a clue why. You walked out on our marriage and left me a four-line-long apology like you'd cancelled a dinner date,' he breathed in raw wonderment. 'It was unreal. I didn't even know where to find you. I almost went out of my mind with worry!'

Hilary was aghast at what he was telling her. 'I never thought…I didn't even suspect that you would feel like that—'

'It *should* have been you who told me the truth about our marriage.'

Recognising the justness of that censure, she hung her head. She had been a coward and she had made excuses for herself. But what all those excuses came down to in the end was the simple fact that she had chosen to save face at his expense. How too could she have been so insensitive that she had not foreseen how her disappearance would affect him?

'I had complete trust in you.' Roel ensnared her troubled gaze when she would have evaded his scrutiny. 'Admittedly that was my only option at first. But our relationship developed fast and I let my guard down with you. I believed we were a couple. I learned to think of you as my wife. Then it all blew up in my face.'

Hilary's throat ached. Ever since he had brought her back from London she had refused to consider how much her own behaviour must have contributed to his angry and cynical distrust. She was ashamed. 'I must have seemed very selfish to you…but I honestly didn't think you'd miss me that much—'

Roel released a humourless shout of laughter. '*Inferno!* What do you think I am? A block of wood?'

'Ice,' she countered unevenly. 'Very self-contained and disciplined and proud of it too.'

·His beautiful mouth twisted. 'I was brought up to be strong and well warned never to make myself vulnerable with a woman. Their failed marriages embittered my father and my grandfather. By the time Clemente changed his tune, it was too late for him to influence me. That was why he made that insane will. It was his last-ditch attempt to persuade me that if I would only make the effort and take the risk I could rewrite family history and end up in a happy marriage.'

'Well…' her nose wrinkled as she fought back the awful tickle of threatening tears '…so much for that hope but at least the *castello* is still in the family.'

'I want you to know that I was already on my way home to see you when Paul contacted me—'

A mortified flush lit her creamy complexion. 'Why do guys always stick together?'

'Mutual terror?' Roel quipped in a roughened undertone, level dark golden eyes welded to her. 'When I understood what sort of agreement you were seeking, I was ashamed. I knew instantly that I had driven you to it.'

Hilary surveyed him with wide, bewildered eyes. 'What is it with you? Why weren't you pleased? Why would you be ashamed? I was willing to sign a declaration saying I would never make a claim on your wealth or anything else you owned!'

'But that would have been wrong because you have every right to share what I have—'

'It would have shown you once and for all that I don't want or need anything from you!'

Roel drew in a ragged breath and squared his broad shoulders. 'I accused you of being a gold-digger because that way I could avoid dealing with how I really felt about you.'

Her brow indented. 'I don't understand.'

'When I had amnesia, I got used to having you around. After I got my memory back, I was furious with you because you had made one hell of a fool of me!'

That frank condemnation leeched colour from below Hilary's skin. 'That wasn't my intention and it isn't how I see what happened between us,' she protested.

'But it changed everything. You'd fooled me successfully and I had no confidence in my own ability to read you after that.' Savage tension emanating from his lithe, powerful frame, Roel swung away from her. 'But no matter how great my distrust of you was, I still wanted you back and *not* only because the sex was dynamite.'

Hilary perked up at that promising confession. 'But you were quite happy for me to think that it was just that.'

His bold bronzed profile clenched as she put him on the spot yet again. 'I was covering up…I was—' He bit off whatever he had been about to say and raised and dropped a broad shoulder in visible frustration. 'I was…'

'You were…what?' she prompted.

'Scared! *OK?*' He shot that reluctant admission at her as if she had turned a gun on him. 'I was scared. I was feeling stuff I'd never felt before and it spooked me. But even by the time we arrived in Sardinia I had simmered down. I was relaxing and beginning to trust you again…'

Hilary opened dry lips. 'Then I admitted I was pregnant—'

'Once again you'd been secretive. If only you had shared that news with me immediately. All that week we had been together and we had been closer than I had ever been with any woman but, throughout it, you'd been hiding the fact that you were carrying our child. That hit me hard, made me wonder what else you might be hiding,' he confessed heavily.

'I was afraid of how you'd react.' But her attempt to defend herself was half-hearted for she could now see that keeping Roel in the dark about her pregnancy had damaged his view of her all over again.

His stunning dark golden eyes held her strained gaze levelly. 'I needed you to be honest. You weren't and I had lost faith in my own judgement. From that point on, everything went haywire—'

'*You*…went haywire,' Hilary slotted in unhappily. 'But I'm not holding that against you. It's not a hanging offence if you don't want a baby you didn't plan to have with me—'

'I *do* want our baby very much. But I was afraid that you were taking me for another ride,' Roel breathed with suppressed savagery. 'I've been at war with myself ever since. Although I was determined to hang onto both of you I hated the idea that you might stay with me solely because you were expecting my child. Does that sound crazy to you?'

'No…I felt the same way,' she muttered ruefully.

'I was trying so hard to stay in control that I went off the rails…' Roel spread lean brown hands in a gesture that denoted honest remorse, dark colour accentuating his hard, handsome features. 'I ended up accusing you of things I didn't even believe. I *knew* the baby was mine but I didn't want you to suspect that you had hurt me again, so I decided to hurt first.'

In receipt of that surprising admission, Hilary listened with even greater concentration. She had hurt him? Had he really said those words?

'I've been fighting what I feel for you ever since and I can't do it any more,' Roel confided hoarsely. 'I've been trying to work up a resistance to you—'

'I'm not a disease…' Hilary whispered.

'Not seeing you was the only thing that worked. Then you came down in that kimono thing for breakfast *and*…I realised I was failing badly in the resistance stakes—'

'You were offensive—'

'I'm sorry. I was angry with myself, not with you. I was furious that I could not control my desire for you. I took refuge in sarcasm. It's an unfortunate defence mechanism.'

'It was the last straw—'

'It won't happen again,' Roel intoned urgently. 'I'm new at all this and it's not easy. Do you think you could give me another chance?'

Her eyes misted over and she shook her head, too worked up to manage a verbal negative.

Roel reached for her clenched hands. *'Please…'*

Again she shook her head. 'I don't want a guy who's just making the best of things with me,' she confided on the back of a sob. 'Or a husband who thinks I'm so much of a second-class citizen he has to fight even fancying me—'

'It's not like that. If it were only sex, I wouldn't have messed up to this extent. I'm at home with sex…it's all this other stuff I'm useless with. Don't you realise how much you mean to me?' Roel held fast to her hands, brilliant dark eyes pinned to her with fierce appeal. 'You said it in Sardinia. You said I was perfectly happy living in your fantasy fairy-tale marriage. You were right…in fact I have never been happier.'

Hilary was so shaken by that admission she gaped at him.

'So possibly you can imagine how I felt when the fairy tale turned out to be a fantasy. I had thought you loved me. I had learned to like that idea—'

'Really?' Her voice came out all squeaky.

'I fell in love with you. But I've never been in love before and, unfortunately, I didn't recognise what was wrong with me—'

'What was *right* with you,' Hilary corrected with helpless stress, hanging eagerly on his every word.

'Well, it didn't feel right at the start,' Roel asserted feelingly. 'You were coming between me and work…'

'Oh, dear…' she said chokily. 'Do I really?'

Roel looked very grave. 'Sometimes my mind wanders to you even in important meetings.'

'That's more than I ever hoped for.' Unashamed tears in her eyes, Hilary slid her arms up round his neck. 'I love you too. I love you so much and I'm going to make you very, very happy.'

He crushed her into an emotional embrace that spoke far louder than any words could have done. For a long time they just stood there wrapped tight in each other's arms, each of them savouring that closeness that they had both feared was gone for ever.

'You make me feel good, *amata mia*,' he muttered a shade gruffly.

'You see—loving me is not all bad news,' she said warmly.

'It is when you keep on disappearing and threatening to leave me,' Roel disagreed.

'I won't ever disappear again and I will never—no matter *how* mad you make me—threaten to leave you again,' she promised solemnly.

He bent his handsome dark head and stole a single, almost unbearably tender kiss that made her entire being light up with loving feelings. His lustrous golden eyes clung to her upturned face. 'I think on some level I knew four years ago that you could be very dangerous to the single lifestyle I cherished, *cara mia*.'

'I was a bit immature for you then. But I did fall for you the first time I saw you.'

'I never admitted it even to myself but I was very strongly attracted to you. That's why I kept on coming back to the salon where you worked.' He kissed her again and her eyes slid dreamily shut. 'Once we'd been through that wedding ceremony, though, I couldn't trust myself anywhere near you—'

'Seriously?'

'Seriously. Marrying you put you off limits but I've been carrying your photograph in my wallet for four years,' Roel murmured ruefully.

Big grey eyes opened wide to take full appreciative note of his discomfiture. She glowed with pleasure.

His lean, intelligent face tender, he looked down at her with immense appreciation. 'I'd love to see you wearing a wedding dress for me. We need to make more of the occasion. We should renew our vows and have our marriage blessed.'

'I'd love that…' she muttered, touched to the heart.
'But you'll have to wait until after the baby's born.'

'Nonsense,' Roel contradicted without hesitation.

Eleven months later, Hilary and Roel renewed their
vows in the atmospheric little chapel only a mile from
the Castello Sabatino.

Hilary carried yellow roses and wore a beautiful
boned brocade bodice teamed with a frothy skirt. The
happy couple only had eyes for each other. A superb
meal and a lively party followed the ceremony. Her
two closest friends, Pippa and Tabby, attended with
their husbands, Andreo and Christien. Paul and Anya
Correro shared the top table, for over the past year
Anya and Hilary had forged as good a friendship as
their respective husbands now enjoyed. Her sister,
Emma, was also present. The guest of honour was
indisputably Pietro, the smallest and newest member
of the Sabatino family. But being barely three months
old and quite unimpressed by the festivities, he slept
through most of the day.

Later that evening, Hilary settled her baby into his
cot in the beautiful nursery, which she had had great
fun furnishing for his occupation. Her son had his
father's black hair and an adorable smile that ensured
he got loads of attention. In that she reckoned he was
rather like his father as well.

She found it hard to credit that she and Roel had
almost reached their first unofficial anniversary and
she smiled to herself, relishing her own sense of security and contentment. They spent a lot of time at
the *castello* where the slower pace of life was more
relaxing. Roel had started travelling less during her
pregnancy and he spoilt her like mad.

'Gorgeous…' Roel pronounced huskily from several feet away.

Hilary bestowed a proud look upon their sleeping son. 'I know he's ours but he really is a good-looking baby, isn't he?'

Roel closed his arms slowly round his wife and turned her to face him. 'It wasn't Pietro I was referring to, *amata mia*.'

'No?' Looking up into his darkly handsome features and the sensual appreciation in his golden eyes, she felt her heartbeat quicken and her mouth ran dry.

'You looked incredibly beautiful today. I was so proud that you are my wife.' His dark, deep drawl exuded unashamed satisfaction. 'Do you realise that this is the equivalent of the wedding night we never had?'

Her knees felt weak and she leant up against him, shamelessly angling for the intoxicating heat of his mouth on hers. With a sexy groan of masculine compliance he kissed her before he carried her down the corridor into their bedroom.

'Still love me?' she whispered, breathless with excitement.

His charismatic smile flashed over her with the special warmth that was hers alone. 'I love you more every day.'

Joy in her heart, she matched those loving words and, lacing her arms round him, she drew him down to her.

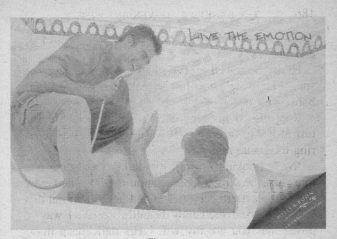
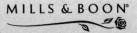

MILLS & BOON®

Live the emotion

Modern Romance™

THE MISTRESS PURCHASE *by Penny Jordan*

Leon Stapinopolous has never known defeat in the
boardroom – or in the bedroom! His acquisition of one
of France's oldest perfume houses is just another notch
in his business profile – but he insists that stunning
perfume designer Sadie Roberts is included in the
purchase price!

THE OUTBACK MARRIAGE RANSOM *by Emma Darcy*

At sixteen, Ric Donato wanted Lara Seymour – but they
were worlds apart. Years later he's a city tycoon, and
now he can have anything he wants... Lara is living a
glamorous life with another man, but Ric is determined
to have her – and he'll do whatever it takes...

A SPANISH MARRIAGE *by Diana Hamilton*

Javier married Zoe purely to protect her from male
predators who were tempted by her money and her
beauty – he has all the money he could ever need. But
as their paper marriage continues he finds it increasingly
hard to resist his wife – even though he made her a
promise...

HIS VIRGIN SECRETARY *by Cathy Williams*

Italian millionaire Bruno Giannella is every woman's
dream. So Katy thinks she must be dreaming when he
demands she become his live-in secretary! But Bruno is
convinced there's a sensual woman hiding beneath Katy's
timid mousy exterior...

On sale 2nd April 2004

*Available at most branches of WHSmith, Tesco, Martins, Borders,
Eason, Sainsbury's and all good paperback bookshops.*

0304/01a

MILLS & BOON

PASSIONATE
PROTECTORS

Lori Foster
Donna Kauffman
Jill Shalvis

Three brand-new novellas
– packed full of danger and desire!

On sale 2nd April 2004

*Available at most branches of WHSmith, Tesco, Martins, Borders,
Eason, Sainsbury's and all good paperback bookshops.*

Live the emotion

PENNINGTON

BOOK TEN

Available from 2nd April 2004

Available at most branches of WHSmith, Tesco, Martins, Borders,
Eason, Sainsbury's and most good paperback bookshops.

PENN/RTL/10

FREE

4 BOOKS
AND A SURPRISE GIFT!

We would like to take this opportunity to thank you for reading this Mills & Boon® book by offering you the chance to take FOUR more specially selected titles from the Modern Romance™ series absolutely FREE! We're also making this offer to introduce you to the benefits of the Reader Service™ —

- ★ FREE home delivery
- ★ FREE monthly Newsletter
- ★ FREE gifts and competitions
- ★ Exclusive Reader Service discount
- ★ Books available before they're in the shops

Accepting these FREE books and gift places you under no obligation to buy; you may cancel at any time, even after receiving your free shipment. Simply complete your details below and return the entire page to the address below. **You don't even need a stamp!**

YES! Please send me 4 free Modern Romance™ books and a surprise gift. I understand that unless you hear from me, I will receive 6 superb new titles every month for just £2.69 each, postage and packing free. I am under no obligation to purchase any books and may cancel my subscription at any time. The free books and gift will be mine to keep in any case.

P4ZEF

Ms/Mrs/Miss/Mr ....Initials ....
BLOCK CAPITALS PLEASE

Surname ....

Address ....

....

....Postcode ....

Send this whole page to:
UK: FREEPOST CN81, Croydon, CR9 3WZ
EIRE: PO Box 4546, Kilcock, County Kildare (stamp required)

Offer valid in UK and Eire only and not available to current Reader Service subscribers to this series. We reserve the right to refuse an application and applicants must be aged 18 years or over. Only one application per household. Terms and prices subject to change without notice. Offer expires 30th June 2004. As a result of this application, you may receive offers from Harlequin Mills & Boon and other carefully selected companies. If you would prefer not to share in this opportunity please write to The Data Manager at the address above.

Mills & Boon® is a registered trademark owned by Harlequin Mills & Boon Limited.
Modern Romance™ is being used as a trademark.
The Reader Service™ is being used as a trademark.